ghost seas

ALSO BY STEVEN UTLEY

COLLECTIONS
The Beasts of Love
Where or When

POETRY
This Impatient Ape
Career Moves of the Gods

ANTHOLOGIES
Lone Star Universe (co-edited with Geo. W. Proctor)
Passing for Human (co-edited with Michael Bishop)

ghost seas

STEVEN UTLEY

TICONDEROGA PUBLICATIONS

for Molly Jane Gardner,
still

Ghost Seas by Steven Utley

First Published by Ticonderoga Publications

Cover Illustration by Joseph Troffimoff

Designed and edited by Russell B. Farr
Typeset in Goudy Old Style and Duality

National Library of Australia
Cataloging-in-Publications entry

>Utley, Steven, 1948–
>Ghost seas

>2nd ed.
>ISBN 9780980353136 (hc)
>1. Short stories, American–20th century
>A813.54

ISBN 978-0-9803531-3-6 (hc)
ISBN 978-0-9803531-4-3 (tpb)

Ticonderoga Publications
PO Box 29 Greenwood
Western Australia 6924

www.ticonderogapublications.com

10 9 8 7 6 5 4 3 2

Contents

Steven Utley's The Golem, Part VI: Now It's Personal

Howard Waldrop

What you hold in your hands is the product of 27 years of toil, sweat, tears and less pleasant stuff. And not for lack of trying, either.

It's hard enough to try to make any kind of living writing short stories; these days it's something novelists do starting out, or aside from, their novels. Big-name-type writers are given scratches behind the ear and a short story collection when they've done especially well with their last two or three damn thick square books.

This is the pure Utley, the stories he wants in here: the first of many plucked from the Great Tree of Work over the last quarter-century, and a swell harvest it is, too.

You've got the stories here in front of you to read. I don't need to say anything about them, except that you're in for some treats.

I've known Steven Utley since some becalmed soul brought him to the Dallas Area Science Fantasy Society meeting in 1970 that was also the farewell party for me, drafted for the Late Unpleasantness in SE Asia. He was, at the time, employed in an unairconditioned 130°F hellhole vinyl-extruding plant.

I went into the Army a struggling fan-boy. Four days into Basic Training, when I was in no condition to enjoy it, I got word I was now a professional writer.

By the time I go out of the Army 18 months later, so was Utley, and so were a lot of my friends.

It was a neat time to be a young SF writer in Texas, full of piss and beans. For one thing, when you finished your own work (and it didn't sell, or sold slowly), you could collaborate with all the other struggling young writers, and together, or three or four of you, wrote stuff that sold first time out, every time.

So what follows is not a bio/bibliography of Steven D. Utley, boy writer guy, but some of the things that come back to me as we slogged our ways through what we with straight faces used to call our careers, mostly, but not all, around Austin TX where Utley still, and I used to, live.

Por exemplo:

I am living on a cot, in an otherwise empty storage room, at Utley's—used to be Joe Pumilia's which used to be Al Jackson's—house, for a couple of months between places, which went across New Year's Eve 1979.

We're running very late. We have cleaned the house for the party. Utley is cooking scones, or somedamnthing or other. He puts on his big asbestos mitt (the kind you use to handle plutonium) and bends down to take the goodies out of the roaring oven on their big baking sheet.

There is a knock on the back door. There is a louder knock on the front door (*nobody* uses the front door!). The phone rings. The dog goes crazy. The cats run around the ceiling. Steven, distracted in his oven mitt, turns first toward one sound, then the other, then another.

He heads toward one of the doors.

"Hold this," he says, and hands me the cookie sheet.

I, also distracted, took it.

Having no oven mitt, it didn't take me long to put it on the ceiling near the cats.

The guests come in to find scones all over the house, and me up to my elbows in a sink full of cold water.

"Gee. I thought you had the other potholder," said Steven.

But it wasn't *all* fun like that. Jumping back in time, like one of his stories:

While still around Dallas, 1973 or so, we were supposed to be in the 100th Anniversary Issue of *Famous Monsters of Filmland*, with the only piece of fiction.

It was, at the time, pretty much akin to paying back old debts, for both of us. One of the things that kept Steven going—moving around as an Air Force brat to exotic places like Okinawa, Tennessee, Kansas—in the late Fifties and early 60s, was *Famous Monsters*. (In our maturity, watching *Matinee* by Joe Dante, another FM alumnus, set in the Florida Keys on a Naval Base during the Cuban Missile Crisis, Utley said "That's my life, up there." The kid in the movie changes countries and schools every year or so. One of the things that keeps the kid's life together was SF and monster movies, and *Famous Monsters*. In those days, all the famous Stevens, Steves and Stephens read it and wrote letters to it—Utley, Spielberg, King.)

Anyway, we'd written a story called "Where I Lodge a Little While". It was supposed to appear in the Big 100th Anniversary Issue, with all the tributes, memorials, letters of congratulations from Harryhausen and Bradbury and such. But suddinkly, as Popeye says, Robert Armstrong and Bruce Cabot (co-stars of *King Kong*) drop like Adams and Jefferson, within a few hours of each other at press time, and, the only piece of fiction, we were bumped to a later issue, with no hoopla.

Our two-page story was one of the kind Ackerman loved, in which the character is revealed, in the last line, to be the Frankenstein monster. When it was finally published in issue #102, the title was changed to "Even The Little Children Know."

And it had two stills from *Ghost of Frankenstein* on the first page.

Speaking of which:

Steven and I wrote, in the early 1970s, "Custer's Last Jump" in five days. (You can read *all* about that in the 1996 Ticonderoga reprint.) Among other things it went back and forth between Terry Carr's *Universe*, for which it was written, and Robert Silverberg's *New Dimensions*, for 4 years, due to the usual mid-70s *contretemps* in the publishing houses, with lots of other people trying to get their hands on the thing, too. But, at one of the points when it was back in Carr's lap, Silverberg, who was writing me back rejecting *yet another* of my solo masterpieces said something like, what I'd really like to see is one of those swell things like you and Utley did with "Custer's Last Jump".

Well, I fired off a letter to Bob, telling him how me and Utley were writing another gosh-wow story of super-science, only literate-like; we were just dying to start it.

It just so happened that Utley was going, for the first and last time, to the Nebula Awards Banquest, that very week, on the West Coast, and I was driving him to the airport. At his place, I said: "If Silverberg says *anything* to you, nod your head and go 'Uh-huh'."

"Why?"

"Just do it!" I said. "And while you're at it, gimme that *Demon From The Flaming Sea* thing you never could finish."

By and by he comes back four days later. "I got there and Silverberg said, 'Gee I sure would like to see that story you and Waldrop are writing.' I nodded my head and said 'Uh-huh'."

"Here." I said, "I worked on some of it while you were gone. Only it's now called "Black as the Pit, From Pole to Pole.", from the poem *"Invictus"* by W.E. Henley, the model for Long John Silver, not *Demon From the Flaming Sea*. I got the Frankenstein monster inside the Hollow Earth, fighting pirates. But *you* gotta get him there, and we gotta put in Pym, and Lovecraft and Burroughs."

At some time in the late 70s, Utley took eight or nine years off writing stories, and not without a couple of dozen provocations, either.

For one thing, seven or eight magazines and anthologies folded, or went gaga, or transmogrified before his very eyes, with ten or eleven stories of his in their inventories. Back came *all the stories*, contracted for but not yet paid for, *all at once.*

Steven took a look around him and said, "Plautus wouldn't put up with this *stercus.*"

Then there was, in quick succession, a mysterious malady, unknown to Utley, science or *juju*, which came one day, made his life living hell for a year or two, then went away. Just like *that*. Just in time for him to bust a disk and have a laminectomy, which filled up the pain void for *another* couple of years.

Through all this, somehow, he worked on comic strips and books starring the Huggybunnies, Count Lagomorpha, Bwana Rocket (based on the late Chad Oliver) and true-romance comics in which it is a guy's job to break women's hearts. ("Joan Smith, eh? Can do, Boss!") (The one he talked about, but didn't do, was the *Classics Illustrated* version of *The Great Ratsby* by F. Scott Fitzgerbil.)

During the daytime, between doctor's appointments, he was working for the State of Texas as a proofreader, and, later, the guy with the magic marker who endlessly drew and redrew lines on the district maps, according to the whims of whatever bunch of nut-cases were in power at the time, and passed new, new, New Redistricting Plans (and they were in Federal Court every time they passed a plan). It was a job with endless vistas of bureaucratic security.

But he left it anyway.

That's because he'd started to write real-live stories again, some of which you're going to read in this book, right where he left off, and, if anything, with even more power, incision and wit than the stuff before he took a break. (The field isn't ready for him now; it sure the hell wasn't ready for him *then*.) He was putting words on paper again, and such words they were, too.

In an early piece I did on Steven, I pretended I'd found him derelict somewhere, and taught him everything he knew. ("This is the letter M, Steven. You'll need it if you write about Mars.")

I needn't have worried.

Utley was born knowing that M was for Mars.

Oso, Washington
April 14, 1997

ghost seas

Ghost Seas

How much farther's it going to be?" Jean demanded, fanning herself with the road map.

"We're almost there," Neal said tiredly.

Jean scowled behind her sunglasses and twiddled the knob on the air-conditioner again. It was useless. West Texas heat had been too much for it. She gave up and glared at the desert. Down the highway, and out upon the baked yellow earth bordering it, pools of cool liquid silver shimmered mockingly.

"So where *is* this place, Neal? I can't see it."

"Soon, honey."

"You've been telling me 'Soon, honey' for the past forty-five minutes."

She saw him tighten his grip on the steering wheel and lock his eyes on a non-existent lake covering the road ahead. When, finally, he did speak again, his voice was flat, dead. The heat of the desert could even sap the vitality from sounds.

"We'll be there in fifteen, twenty minutes. No more than that. I promise. I know this road. I've been making this drive for years."

The desert swept past on either side. The waters that were not sparkled in the distance.

"I don't know who's craziest," Jean muttered. "Your Uncle Piper for living in this godforsaken place, you for dragging me out here, me for *letting* you drag me out here."

Neal gave her a wan grin. "You'll like it when we get there, I know you will. And you'll like Uncle Piper. I think he'll like you, too."

"Okay. Okay." She returned the grin. "I'm sorry. It's hot, and I'm tired, and my bottom hurts from sitting on it non-stop from San Antonio."

"We'll be there shortly, and then you can stretch your muscles. And have something to drink."

"And wash." Jean used her finger to trace a line in the dust on the dashboard. "I feel all gritty."

Neal nodded and shifted in his seat. "Me, too."

"You think it'd bother your uncle if we took a bath together?"

He shot her an arch look. "You 'n' me 'n' him?"

"Just you 'n' me, dodo. Uncle Piper can just find someone else to take a bath with. Or are we going to be the only three people for miles and miles in any direction?"

"For all practical purposes."

"I was afraid of that."

Neal swerved the car slightly to avoid running over a large dead animal on the road. "There's a dinky little desert community about seven, eight miles past Uncle's place. Burnick. A grocery store, a filling station, and precious little else. And Angleton's about thirty miles beyond that. Angleton's a real metropolis. There are *two* filling stations there."

"How can people live in places like that? Or are they all crazy old rich people like Uncle Piper?"

"Crazy, maybe. But not rich."

Jean rolled her head from side to side, trying to ease the ache in the muscles of her neck, and, beside her, Neal pressed a little harder on the accelerator.

When they came within sight of Neal's uncle's house, Jean felt relieved. Her husband had told her only that his favorite relative lived in a large old house located in the arid West Texas wilderness, and she had been expecting to see a two-story clapboard affair with peeling white paint, sagging front porch, and, perhaps, antiquated gasoline pump in the front yard.

Uncle Piper's house may have been old, but it had been built to last, built with care and money. It was low and solid-looking, all weathered brick and stone. Gnarled desert trees surrounded it. There was a new pick-up truck parked to one side of the house.

"You can always spot a *real* Texas millionaire," Neal said as he pulled the car off the road, into the dubious shade provided by the trees. "He drives a pick-up, wears blue jeans and cowboy boots, and he doesn't look any different from guys who make sixty bucks a week busting their humps as cowhands." He killed the motor, braced his hands against the steering wheel, and arched his spine. "So what do you think of the real Golden West now?"

"It *is* a bit less grim-looking than I'd imagined."

"Ready?"

"Let's go."

They got out of the car. Jean winced at the return of circulation to her buttocks. Neal came around the car and took her by the hand, and as they started to approach the house, the front door opened, and Uncle Piper stepped out.

He was old. He was old only as those who have been aged by sand and heat can be old. He was reed-thin, the color of ancient leather, with bones that raised hard, sharp ridges under the skin of his cheeks, chin, and hands. A few wisps of brilliantly white hair clung to the top of his skull. His ears were small, shrivelled, and lay flat against his head.

"Neal," he called out in a thin, high voice. "Neal."

Neal quickened his stride. Jean had to take a hopping step to stay abreast of him. She felt his hand slip out of hers and watched, strangely touched, as her husband gave the old man a careful hug. Something glittered in the sunlight. She stared at the gold ring on Uncle Piper's finger.

"I'm glad you've come," the old man said, looking over his nephew's shoulder at Jean. She gave him what she hoped was a dazzling smile. "And who's this you brought with you?"

"Uncle Piper, this is my wife Jean."

"Your wife?" A teakwood-hard hand enveloped hers. She was amazed by the firmness of the grip. The old man's watery blue eyes appraised her from the centers of labyrinths of deep wrinkles. "Well, I'm sure proud to meet you, Jean."

"Neal's told me a lot about you," she said, wondering whether she, too, was supposed to embrace Uncle Piper.

The old man made an amused sound in the back of his throat and let go of Jean's hand. "You two must be tired from your trip. Come on in the house where it's cool. You can sit and have something to drink."

Jean followed the two men through the cool gloom of the house, grateful for the drop in temperature and the absence of glare. The low rumble of air-conditioning units filled her ears. She heard the old man speak to her husband but did not understand what was said. She looked at furniture, pictures, bric-a-brac, without actually seeing them.

They emerged onto a glass-enclosed verandah at the rear of the house. An air conditioner rattled in its window frame. Uncle Piper indicated armchairs and a small refrigerator.

"Excuse me if I tell you to help yourself," he said, "but—"

"Of course," said Neal, guiding Jean to a chair. Uncle Piper sat down beside her. "What would you like to drink, honey?"

"I don't care, as long as it's wet."

The old man leaned toward her and touched the arm of her chair. "I think I got pretty much anything you'd want. Cokes and ice water in the 'frigerator there, tea and coffee in the kitchen. Uh, you drink beer?"

"No." Jean shook her head. "I don't like the taste."

"Just as well. Young lady like you shouldn't drink beer."

Jean repressed a frown. "Neal, I'd like some ice water, please."

"Sure." Neal looked at his uncle and cocked an eyebrow.

"The same." Uncle Piper settled back into his chair. "Well, how you been doing? How's the family and all?"

Neal handed out tumblers full of water. "Apart from the wife you now see before you, I'm doing about what I was the last time I came out. Learning how to be a crackerjack insurance salesman."

"Ah. And the folks?"

"Dad's still doing fine in real estate. You know Mom. Same as ever. Busy with her church groups and PTA meetings."

Uncle Piper snickered softly. "Hear much about your other uncles?"

"Well, Uncle Wilmer's supposed to go into the hospital for another operation next month, but he doesn't want to do it. Aunt Betty's having a fit, of course. And..."

Jean sipped her drink and, unmindful of Neal's droning account of uncles and cousins and others whose relation to the two men with her could only be guessed, stared out across the desert beyond the verandah. There was a hint, a shadow, a faint suggestion, of mountains low on the horizon. A single cloud slowly drifted across the bright blue sky. Lakes shimmered and dissolved, inconsistent shorelines receded before glistening mercury tides. She heard Uncle Piper shift in his chair, heard the air conditioner cough to itself, heard ice cubes tinkle against glass. She watched the phantom tides roll in across the desert, and she wondered why anybody wealthy enough to go wherever and do whatever he chose would opt for such isolation.

Uncle Piper, she had been informed by her husband, had been the first of eleven children. Neal's father had been the eleventh. Eleven children in how many years? Twelve? Fifteen? The thought made her shudder.

Then she heard Neal mention her name. She tore her gaze from ghost seas, her thoughts from speculation about crazy old men, and forced herself to listen.

"...married about a month ago," Neal was saying. "We've moved into Aunt Sarah's old house near Trinity."

Uncle Piper nodded, apparently satisfied with his nephew's account, and leaned toward Jean again. "Might as well tell you, Neal's the only one of my relatives I'm partial to any more. Him and Glen Alvin—you met his cousin Glen Alvin yet? Those two used to come out here every summer, spend a month at a time with me. Heh. Remember the time you almost stepped on that sidewinder, Neal? And Glen Alvin grabbed around for a rock to hit it with and got hold of a cactus instead? Heh. Glen Alvin never did have a whole lot of sense." He snorted softly. "But, like I was saying, Neal's the only one who comes to visit me any more. All the others, I guess they got tired of waiting for me to die."

Jean looked at him dumbly, unable to think of a reply. Her embarrassment must have been obvious, for the old man gave her a kindly smile and patted her arm.

"Neal's never sucked up to me, Jean. He's a good boy who cares about a crazy old man. Not like the rest of the brood. Bunch of damn vultures, every one of them."

Neal set his glass down atop the refrigerator. "Look," he said, "I'd better get the suitcases out of the car before they melt. Then, Uncle, if you'll let me have my wife back for a few minutes, we need to get cleaned up."

"Of course."

"And then I could make dinner," Jean said. "I can't promise you that you'll like whatever I fix. But it'd probably be different, at least."

"Heh. 'Most anything'd be an improvement over my cooking." Uncle Piper waved Neal into the house and got up to walk to the door of the verandah. Jean studied the back of his wrinkled neck while he seemed to study the desert. "You might wonder," he said after a moment, "what a man who made himself a millionaire by the time he was thirty-five is doing holed up in a place like this."

"Yes. I was wondering."

He turned and smiled crookedly. "Well, then, I'll tell you. Enough folks already think I'm crazy without you being one of them. I worked like the devil to make all that money. When I got it, I high-rolled with the best of them for a while. Had me a big house in Houston, another one in Dallas, more cars than I could keep track of. I was one of the first men in the state to have more than one privately owned airplane. Oh, I did me some high living, all right. But you get to an age when you realize you better take it slow and easy. So I came out here, twenty, twenty-five years it's been now, and I built this house, and then I sat down in it to catch my breath. Do a little reading, you know, something I never had much time for. A little reading and a lot of thinking. Desert's a good place for thinking about things like death and immortality."

He chuckled and turned back toward the desert. "That's providing, of course, you got somewhere to get in out of the sun. The desert's mighty particular about letting a person live in it. You don't take it seriously, it'll find ways to kill you. You believe in it, it lets you live forever. So I just sit here, and I think and watch those mirage lakes dance. And, nights, I hear them lapping against the bricks outside my bedroom window. Like the desert'd decided to become a sea again."

"Again?"

"Um hmm. This all used to be the bottom of a sea. Millions and millions of years ago. I read that in a book someplace."

"What happened to it? The sea, I mean."

Uncle Piper fingered the rim of his glass. "Oh, it just went away. But I think it keeps trying to come back. Those lakes that aren't there— that's the old sea, trying to come back."

Jean heard Neal call to her above the noise of the air conditioner. She set her glass aside and rose. Uncle Piper looked at her intently and shook his head. His voice was soft and sad.

"Crazy old men think crazy thoughts, don't they?"

By the time the three of them had eaten Jean's dinner, the sky was beginning to darken. The temperature plummeted sharply. The old man moved through his house, switching off air conditioners.

While Neal busied himself in the spare bedroom, Jean washed the dishes. She was drying the last plate when Uncle Piper entered the kitchen.

He watched her put the plate away, then said, "You know, there's times I wish I'd married."

"Why didn't you?"

He shrugged. "I guess I was just too busy trying to get rich when I was young. And too busy *being* rich when I was middle-aged. Now I'm too old, and I've been out here too long. There's things here I take for granted that a wife'd never learn to live with."

"Then you should've married someone who grew up in the desert."

"Nobody grows up in the desert, Jean. Old, but not up."

"You're making fun of me," she chided gently.

"Oh, no," Uncle Piper said slowly, "not at all. Gospel truth. Only old folks live in places like Burnick and Angleton. They live there 'cause they have to. They believe in those ghost seas out there on the sand, and believing the sea's going to come back is like believing in the afterlife."

Jean shivered in spite of herself. They looked out through the kitchen window. The sun was almost below the horizon. In the gathering darkness, she thought that she saw something gleam and ripple like liquid silver.

That night, she dreamed of warm green waters and smooth-skinned creatures that stretched serpentine necks above the surface and gazed up at unknown constellations.

The following day, she accompanied Neal and Uncle Piper on a walk into the desert. She returned to the house tired, blistered, and bored. She made lunch and let the old man make dinner. She made polite conversation for as long as she could. She made a face at her husband, behind his back, and retired to the parlor when he and his uncle sat down on the verandah to talk about nothing in particular.

Neal came to her after about thirty minutes. She had a book lying open in her lap and a frown frozen on her face. Her husband walked over to her and gave her a kiss on her left temple and tried to sound cheerful when he said, "What's up, honey?"

Jean closed the book very deliberately and looked at her hands. "Neal, I'm sorry, but I'm going to be climbing the walls if we stay the other two days here."

He knelt beside her chair and took one of her hands in his. "Can't you find something interesting to do?"

"What *is* there to do?"

"You could always read," he said drily.

Jean scowled at him.

"Or you could watch television," he went on. "All the comforts and conveniences of the late twentieth century are at your disposal."

"Oh, *screw* television." Jean looked at him imploringly. "Neal, I'm bored, bored out of my mind. I don't like it here. I'm sorry, but I don't like it here."

Neal sighed harshly. "Honey, Uncle Piper's a nice old man who's glad for our company. He likes you. He told me so. Come on, join us on the verandah, and we'll all have a nice talk. Don't be anti-social."

"I'm tired of sitting on the verandah and twiddling my thumbs and looking at the desert." It was her turn to sigh. "Okay. He's a nice old man. But I have nothing to say to him."

"Sweetheart, don't be this way."

"How am I supposed to be? You bring me out here to the middle of nowhere, set me down with nothing to do, and then you expect me to thoroughly enjoy myself. I can't even go to a movie. They've probably never even *heard* of movies in Burnick."

Neal's expression hardened somewhat. "Maybe you need to go lie down for a while. You're still tired from this morning, and it's making you cranky."

"I'm not tired and cranky," she snapped. "I'm bored and cranky, and there's a difference. I want to go home, where there're things to do, people I can talk to."

"Go lie down, Jean. A nap—"

"*Neal.*"

"—will do you good. Go on. Uncle Piper will understand."

"I'm sure he will."

"Look, damn it, be good!"

"Don't yell at me."

"I wasn't yelling at you."

"You did."

Neal's face contorted with sudden rage. "Don't *ruin* it, Jean!"

She stared at him, frightened by the fury boiling just beneath the surface of his voice, and she was an instant away from asking him, *Ruin what?*, when something clicked in her mind.

Rich old Uncle Piper. Devoted nephew Neal.

Neal's never sucked up to me, Jean.

Neal's the only one of my relatives I'm partial to any more.

Rich old Uncle Piper, devoted nephew Neal.

Jean placed the book on the lamp table and got to her feet. She heard her husband exhale loudly, obviously exasperated, but she did not look at him. She took a step and paused to regard the contents of the little glass display case on the coffee table for a moment. The case was filled with odd bits of desert debris, fossilized sea shells, petrified trilobites. Flotsam from prehistoric times.

She left the room and went to bed.

She was forced to admit to herself that it did indeed feel good to stretch out between cool, clean sheets. She lay with her eyes closed and savored the darkness. The bedroom door was shut, but she could hear indistinct murmurings from the verandah and knew that the two men were once again gazing out into the night, discussing, perhaps, unreal waters. She trembled, rolled over onto her side, and hugged the pillow.

She missed San Antonio and city lights and the muted rumble of traffic. She missed her friends. She missed all of the things that made life interesting, all of the things that did not, could not, exist in the desert. She had come to Texas from the Tennessee heartland, where it was cool and green, and before Neal brought her to see Uncle Piper she had never been farther west than San Antonio. The vastness and emptiness of the desert depressed her. Uncle Piper depressed her. Neal depressed her.

She fell asleep hating the sand, the sun, the glare, dusty roads, the baking heat that radiated from the surfaces of deep, wet optical illusions.

Sometime after midnight, Jean awoke with a terrible thirst. The room was still and quiet, suffused with moonlight. She got out of bed, taking care not to disturb her sleeping husband, slipped into her robe, and padded noiselessly to the kitchen to get herself a drink of water.

She was on her way back to bed when she heard a sound from the direction of the verandah: *slap, slap; slap.* She paused in the hall, trying to decide what it might be.

The air conditioner.

The wind in the trees outside.

The house settling, speaking to itself.

She went out onto the verandah.

Beyond the glass-enclosed porch, the sea glistened in the moonlight, and long-necked things with iridescent skins regarded her hungrily.

Jean's breath caught in her throat. She ground the heels of her palms into her eyes and looked again.

The night lay upon the desert. Faintly, very faintly, an animal cried out.

She went to the door, unlocked it, and stepped out onto the cold stone steps. The hateful desert was silent.

The land of death and bleached skulls, she thought. The land of treachery and deception....

"Jean?"

She gasped and half-turned. Neal stood behind her on the verandah.

"I woke up and found you gone," he said. "What're you doing out here?"

"I..." She shook her head helplessly.

"Come on back to bed, honey. Before you wake Uncle."

Jean felt the muscles in her jaw jerk taut. "Your show of concern for a rich old man is touching."

His eyes widened. "What?"

"Your devotion, Neal. Your incredible devotion. How... how long ago was it you dedicated your time to becoming his favorite nephew? How did you come by such patience and determination?"

"What're you talking about?"

"I'm talking about you coming out here every three months or so, putting up with his craziness. Doing everything you could to convince him that you sincerely care about him. That you love his stinking desert as much as he does. What was it he said? About the rest of his relatives giving up hope of him ever dying?"

"Come to bed." Neal's voice was ragged with barely contained anger. "Come on now."

"You must hate it here even more than I do. Isn't that right? You only put up with it, and with him, because you know he's going to leave you everything. You *know*."

"Shut *up*."

"*It's true, isn't it?*"

Neal lunged forward, arms outstretched, mouth opened in a soundless yell, and, at the same instant, something warm and wet tickled Jean's foot. Startled, she jerked the foot away and lost her balance. Her husband's hand closed around her wrist. Then they hit the water together, screaming.

Something feathery brushed her thigh as they sank. She flailed at Neal. The water filled her nose and mouth, stung her eyes, poured into her and bore her down. Soft mud squished between her toes and swirled about her calves as she kicked and thrashed on the bottom.

Neal's hand squeezed her wrist painfully, relaxed, let go.

Jean put her feet against the bottom and pushed herself up to the surface. The sea disgorged her and left her lying on the hard, dry earth, gasping for air, shivering with cold and terror. She may have shrieked. She may have called her husband's name. She may have made no sound at all as darkness closed over her as completely as any sea.

When she awoke, she was in the high brass bed in the guest room. She raised her head slightly and, through the window, saw gnarled trees rippling in the heat. She felt chilled.

"Jean," said Uncle Piper.

Jean looked at him, a brown, brittle husk of a human being perched upon a chair against the wall opposite the window. His chin was quivering.

"What happened?" she gasped. Her mouth tasted salty. Something gritted between her molars. "Where's Neal?"

Uncle Piper shook his head sorrowfully. "Don't move from that bed. I called the doctor from Angleton. Should be here soon. Don't you move from that bed until he says it's okay for you to."

"Where's Neal?"

"Jean."

"*Where is he?*"

The old man puffed out his leathery cheeks and stared down at his lap. "I'm sorry, I'm real sorry. I loved that boy. I'm sorry."

Tears gathered under her eyelids. She turned away from the old man and pressed her face into the pillow. When, after several minutes, she stopped crying, she realized that Uncle Piper had left the room.

She sat up on the edge of the bed and listened to the rumble of the air conditioner for a moment before standing, then glanced down at her feet. They were encrusted with dried mud.

"Oh, oh, my God."

She heard the verandah door slam shut and moved painfully across the room, out into the hall, out onto the glass-walled back porch. The old man was standing twenty feet away from the house, arms spread, head thrown back, mouth open in a grimace of agony.

"Damn you!" she heard him screech. "*Damn you!*"

And as she watched Uncle Piper stagger away into the dry, shrivelling heat, howling, striking the air with his fists, cursing the desert and its mirror-bright patches of phantom water, warm green prehistoric waves began to break and eddy about his knees.

The Tall Grass

Moody must be dead. The last I saw of him, he was kneeling at the bow. I don't know what happened to him, I had problems aft, in the pilot's high-chair, but I imagine that he turned at the sound of my scream, and probably started to rise, and then he was pitched forward, overboard, directly into the path of the swamp-glider as it struck that mass of fallen tree-ferns. He's probably pinned underneath the wreckage, probably smashed all to hell, too. The hull rotors would've given him a thorough working-over. He should have been in his seat, should have had his belt on. But, then, I was in my seat and had my belt on, and still am and do, and got smashed all to hell just the same. And there's no way Moody could have known, or would ever have thought, that I could be so stupid as to keep one hand on the throttle and take the other from the tiller.

I thought I heard the helicopter pass over the area about half an hour ago but couldn't raise anybody on my helmet radio. The helicopter gave no sign of having located us and hasn't returned. I take this to mean that the beacon transmitter isn't functioning, and that, orange hull or no, the swamp-glider is hidden from view from above. Some of the scaly-boled growths here reach heights of thirty meters; those along the undercut banks of this stream lean out over the water, and their tangly tops form a sort of Gothic arch of greenery.

I don't think Moody and I are going to be found today. Tomorrow will be too late. Today is already too late for him, of course, and will be too late for me in another twenty-eight minutes. I have that much oxygen left, and about that much daylight, too. The days are short here. The Earth spins faster on its axis. This is the last day of my life, and I'm being shortchanged.

If I could move my arms and use my hands, I could get my helmet off and go on breathing, into the night. Regulations are pretty emphatically against it. "Never open your suit." Still, I could hardly contaminate the place as much as Moody already has. I couldn't be harmed as much as I have already been harmed. I'd get to smell the probably rank and yeasty Devonian Period. Later, of course, when my painkillers had worn off, I could just hang here in my tilted chair and scream as I rotted away from the navel down.

Jesus, think about something *else!*

Okay.

Well. You'd think that I would spend such little time as remains to me either praying to God that I get out of this mess alive or else making my peace with Him. But God hasn't been invented yet. You'd think that I would be cataloging my own effects, so to speak, going down the list of my great regrets. But I have only one great regret right now, and it is that I am not going to get out of this mess alive. You'd think that I would think about home, or the people I've loved and by whom been loved, or the high points of my long and, I trust, valuable career. This, unfortunately, is the high point of my career, or was meant to be, anyway. It's certainly one hell of a culmination. I could appreciate the humor of it were it happening to one of my rivals.

And I can conjure up, not homey scenes or people's names and faces, but only Naha Air Force Base, Okinawa, in 1959, and myself as I was there and then, a ten-year-old boy with a burr haircut. And why not? At age ten, I have no regrets, most people but especially all women are a source of irritation and confoundment to me, I have no idea what I should grow up to be, I have no idea that I am to die far from Okinawa and very far from 1959. In fact, I have no idea that I am going to die anywhere at any time. Death, as I understand it at the time, is going to happen to people in the future as it has happened to people in the past, but doesn't happen to people in the present.

Supporting this notion are the facts that nobody I know has actually died, and that Okinawa, fourteen years earlier, was taken by the Americans from the Japanese, at horrific cost of life to both sides and, as well, to the not-quite-Japanese Okinawans, who got caught in the middle. Give me a break, I'm ten years old.

The Japanese Army, with the help of conscripted Okinawan laborers, dug tunnels and sniper-holes and artillery emplacements all over the southern end of the island, then dared all comers. Sitting among the barracks near my house at Naha AFB is an old concrete gun bunker, with the gun still on its mounts. Everyone who has entered the bunker since the summer of 1945 has scratched a name or initials or a message on the oxidizing barrel. The street I live on lies between two steep ridges that are riddled with tunnels and hidey-places. Occasionally, you find old ordnance lying about in these. Very occasionally, you find human bones. My best friend, who lives just up the block from me, has found a skull in the tall grass that grows wild along the base of the ridge at his end of the street. His parents take it away from him; though. Maybe they bury it. Maybe they throw it into a garbage can.

Every adult American finds Okinawa scary. You start to get the idea that the island is death's own stalking ground before you even leave the States: everyone in the family has to be inoculated against every disease known to science. You get to the island and find it teeming with other hazards. You're told not to eat the food or drink the water in the villages which are indoor-plumbing-less, and that it's not a good idea to have too much to do with the Okinawans, beyond hiring them as gardeners and maids. Every American household seems to have a maid named either Fujiko or Fumiko, who speaks vastly better broken English than nearly any American can speak broken Japanese. The humidity is such that your drapes rot overnight. The salt air corrodes your automobile. When the novelty of being in a foreign land that you can drive from one end of to the other in two hours has worn off, you can only go "home," to a housing development on base that is designed to make you think you're living in a typical suburban community back home, save for the houses being built to withstand typhoons. At "home," you can worry about Communist China, sitting just the other side of the East China Sea from you, waiting for you to relax your vigilance. You can wonder if Fujiko talks about you in Japanese to Fumiko next door. You can become an alcoholic.

Every teenaged American just finds Okinawa boring.

Every ten-year-old male American is at war with every female American of any age—I am, anyway—but girls can be avoided and mothers eluded by the simple expedient of heading into the high bamboo. I have, besides a mother, three sisters who are older than me but not so much older that they are above making my life a living hell. I was at a disadvantage back in the States, outnumbered, much put-upon, trapped in a thoroughly tamed, sane, safe, sterile world in which I found no refuge from coziness, no outlet for my wild boyness. Okinawa changes everything. My mother and especially my sisters hate it. I love it. It is a storehouse of treasures to me, and the best playground I have ever had. I start exploring the possibilities at once. I ride my bicycle everywhere, look at and crawl upon and into everything, join the Boy Scouts, sleep out of doors, return home tired and grinning and dirty beyond my wildest hopes and my mother's worst nightmares.

For a time, that great graffiti-encrusted gun is my favorite object on the island. Crouched behind it, I lob thousands of silent, invisible, death-dealing shells implausible distances at impossible trajectories. The severely handled Commie invasion fleet is sent limping home to mainland China.

Then I find the B-29s parked behind the flight line, three or four of them, the last ones in the United States Air Force inventory, now engineless hulks gutted of instruments and used only in firefighting drills. I crawl all through the legendary Superfort's belly, man the tail-gunner's cramped box to drive off a swarm of Zeroes and MiGs, man the bombardier's station, peer, aim, annihilate.

And I ride my bicycle past the gate and out of Naha AFB to the Naha waterfront, where I see a dead whale being expertly flensed by men armed with halberd-like implements. I explore the reefs at low tide, marvel at the bristly sea urchins in their entrenchments, daring all comers, marvel when a sea cucumber ejects its stomach at me as I wade past, marvel as an eel emerges from its lair beneath a rocky shelf and conducts a quick, professional reconnaissance of its tidal pool.

And there are the tunnels, which you're not supposed to enter, and the old ordnance, which you're not supposed to go near, and the bones, which you're not supposed to touch. And I revel in doing all of these forbidden things.

It's all tall grass and horror to girls and mothers. They won't venture near such things, and try to keep you away from them, too. They threaten you with habu bites. But I fear nothing that hasn't any legs. They threaten you with centipede stings, and I repress a shudder, centipedes have entirely too many legs, but damned if I'll let even centipedes keep me out of the tall grass. That's where the choicest delights are. Treasures always have monsters to guard them.

Habus are the lesser monsters, centipedes, the greater.

Habu is the Okinawans' generic term for any of a variety of indigenous venomous serpents; it has virtually replaced *snake* in the lexicon of Americans as well, for it is not only quite serviceably emphatic ("habu!") but cute, too. The only habus I ever see are coiled-up ones preserved in jars of formaldehyde at the Quonset hut where my Boy Scout troop musters. They are used as visual aids in the scoutmaster's standard lecture on safety in the tall grass. He delivers the lecture on the eve of our every camping trip. "Now, boys," he says, "if you're bitten by a habu, there're antivenins available. But each kind of habu venom has to be countered with the right kind of antivenins. So remember—*kill* the habu and *bring* it *in*."

It isn't just Boy Scouts who are told this. Over dinner one evening, my father, an Air Force sergeant, regales me and horrifies everyone else with the true story of an Airman 3rd in his unit who was bitten by a habu while chopping weeds in a ditch. This Airman 3rd had the presence of mind to remember the safety lectures and went after the snake with proper determination and had it in hand, properly defunct, when he arrived at the emergency room. He was mad as hell, too, having sustained an additional six bites in the extinguishing of that poor reptile. "Getting mad saved his life," my father concludes. "All that adrenaline."

This story serves the useful function of defanging habus for me: they are never afterward a source of more than mild concern.

Centipedes are another matter.

Centipedes look like things that would be kept as pets by the tubey, tentacly alien invaders in *I Married a Monster From Outer Space*, a movie I watch three times in two days at the Naha AFB theatre. The scout-master, when he has finished telling us about habus, brings out, the jar containing the centipede. It is the *pièce de résistance*.

"Now, boys," the scoutmaster says, "if you're walking in the tall grass and a centipede drops onto your arm, *don't* swat it. *Flick it off.*"

He demonstrates the technique of flicking. I'm unconvinced that the impact of my own index-fingertip would register on a ten-inch-long-centipede, let alone propel it from my person.

"All you'll do if you swat a centipede on your arm," the scoutmaster continues, "is drive its poison-tipped legs right into you. So always remember—*flick*, don't *swat*."

Flick, don't swat. You'd think it would be easier to remember than "red on yellow, friendly fellow."

But the centipede, all barbed and spiny and strangely waxy-looking, as though it had been crafted from melted-down black and orange crayons, is absolutely the most terrifying thing I have ever seen. I just know that if such a monster were to drop onto my arm, I wouldn't have the presence of mind to remember to flick, not swat. And what if it doesn't drop onto my arm but drops onto my head instead and wraps itself around my face? What if it drops onto my back, and the kid behind me doesn't have the presence of mind to remember to flick, not swat?

The first few times I go into the bamboo after having had my first look at the monster in the jar (for go I must, monsters or no), I go like a hunted beast, scouting every turn in the path, every overhanging mass of foliage, ever-watchful for the signs of an ambush. No trap is ever sprung on me, though, and fear becomes by quick turns only wariness, then only alertness. The scoutmaster's pickled specimen is the only centipede I encounter during my Okinawan sojourn.

And it turns out that, even before I return with my family to the States, the monster in the jar begins to fascinate me rather more than it repels me. I come to regard it as just an interesting animal, like the dead whale, like the eel and the echinoderms. All of these become so endlessly interesting to me, in fact, that I begin to read about them. One thing leads to another. Twenty years later, I have a PhD in marine biology, and I am pursuing a second PhD in invertebrate paleontology. Half a century later, I am asked, not at all jokingly, if I want to study living trilobites, ammonites, and eurypterids.

So here I am, back in the tall grass again, in a manner of speaking. This time it seems I am in for keeps. Not that there's actually any grass here, tall or otherwise. Angiosperms haven't been invented yet. Ditto, girls and mothers and habus. Well, mothers, yes, girls, sort of. Sex has been invented. The fishes announced today that they're on the brink of startling and revolutionary breakthroughs in the field of leg and lung development. Until they get some last little problems licked, however, the land belongs to the arthropods. Silverfish- and springtail-like forms abound. So, too, the things that prey upon them, not-quite-spider forms and those already-modern-looking, always-prehistoric-looking exemplars of arachnid ferocity, the scorpions. And centipedes.

I still haven't seen living trilobites and ammonites. I'm never going to get to see them now. We were going to head for the coast tomorrow where these bayous drain equatorial Llanoria's northern flank into the inundated Ouachita geosyncline. I did so want to go diving in those shallows. Knobloch joked about wanting to spearfish for big ugly placoderms with a rocket-launcher. The bed of the Ouachita seaway will one day form the spine of the Ouachita mountain range. The mountain range will one day lie buried under Texas. Me, too.

They *have* to find us and take us back, of course. Regulations are pretty emphatic on that point. "Leave *nothing* behind." Not footprints, not nothing nohow. Can't have the remains of two human beings and a swamp-glider turning up among the fossilized horsetails and seed-ferns. Our proper matrix is sometime around nine o'clock in the evening of December 2, 2008, which was two days ago and three hundred-fifty- or -sixty-odd million years from now. Some of Moody is going to stay behind, and everyone in 2008 is going to be sick with dread over the effect the injection of my dead associate's substance into the local food chain will have. But how can it matter? Protein is only protein. The past is only the past.

I don't envy whoever gets the job of collecting whatever's left of Moody.

Six, seven minutes' oxygen left now. Time flies.

The painkillers are holding up, just barely. Wish I had more, but the suit's first-aid pack has shot its tiny bolt. I felt it automatically jab me in the neck about one half second before what felt like a napalm burst spread across my lap. The suit realized that I had been hurt before I did. Good old science and technology. First B-29s, then time machines, now this. I'm experiencing some moderate discomfort in the groin, a persistent itchy burning sensation. Farther down than that, I feel nothing, which, under the circumstances, is just as well. The drugs are keeping me calm. I feel pretty pleasantly goofy for a man who's about to run out of air.

The light is fading fast now, but I think I just caught a glimpse of some big arthropod as it swam by my feet, which have been dangling in the water all this time. I'd pull them out if I could, but, then, if I could do that, I could do all sorts of other wonderful things, too. I might even be able to get out of this mess alive. Well, I'm not too worried about attracting attention from below. My hermetic longjohns are self sealing. I'm not dripping blood into the water or anything. Besides, the swimmers and the bottom-dwellers have Moody to occupy them. Should be more than enough of him to last them all night.

I'm sorry. I shouldn't be making light of Moody's situation. It's the drugs. It's shock. It's disbelief. It's embarrassment. I have to laugh to keep from crying. Moody and I were friends. We came out here, back here, into the high bamboo, where the treasures are, where monsters who are themselves treasures stand guard. Where, for the first and only time, I lost my head and, so, lost him his life and me mine. I swung the swamp-glider close to one bank to avoid a tangle of fallen boles lying against the other. Then I screamed, let go of the tiller with my left hand, jerked hard on the throttle with my right, as a centipede longer than my arm fell out of the overhanging greenery and landed right in my lap. How stupid of me. And you'd think that, after all this time, I would have had the presence of mind to remember to flick, not swat.

The Dinosaur Season

Angstrom awoke feeling as ancient and dried up as the Mesozoic Era itself. He was of good Scandinavian stock, but more than a quarter-century's worth of dinosaur seasons spent under broiling suns had turned his fair skin the color of old brick. This morning, he felt the weight of every second of those seasons, and he thought worriedly, Am I coming down with whatever Terry's got? Not *now*, please.

He listened to the soft, moist snores emanating from the lump on the other bed. You aren't getting sick, Ang, he told himself, you're just not getting enough sleep. He could not remember having spent a worse night in a motel. Terry's trips from bed to bathroom and back had kept him teetering on the edge of consciousness deep into the small hours of the night. Angstrom swung his bare legs over the side of the bed, stretched his arms high over his head, yawned. He felt brittle with fatigue.

He had just made up his mind not to wake Terry when the snoring lump gave a grunt and a heave and resolved itself into a bleary-eyed young man.

"Time to get up," Terry said in a thick voice.

"For me it is. You stay in bed." Angstrom leaned over him and lightly touched his forehead. It was hot against his fingertips. "No way I'm letting you spend the day in the sun. Go back to sleep."

"Brian needs me."

"Go back to sleep."

"Znot fair," Terry murmured, but he let his head sink back into his pillow and almost immediately began to snore again.

Angstrom took a quick shower and dressed for a hard day in the field. Old shirt, old pants, old shoes, he thought as he studied himself in the mirror. Old man. He stepped out of the room into the open-air sauna of a Central Texas summer's day. It was only eight o'clock in the morning, but the air was already hot and heavy with humidity. Welcome to the Lone Star Steambath.

The motel sat at the edge of town, looking forlorn and excluded. The town itself looked as if it had been half asleep since the end of World War II. A University of Texas van sat in the motel parking lot, and as Angstrom entered the coffee shop he saw a waitress setting breakfast before George and Sally at a table by the big front window. There was no one else in the place. He sat down next to Sally and said, "Just get in?"

George shrugged and speared a sausage on his plate. "Just long enough ago to order breakfast. We finished setting up the horse exhibit real late last night, grabbed an hour or two's sleep, left Austin just as rosy-fingered dawn was pushing back the night."

Sally spread jam on a biscuit half and said, "Carol Harkavy *wasn't* happy about having to hang around so late."

"Just so long as she's happy with the exhibit." Angstrom ordered breakfast for himself, then sat back in his chair and smothered a yawn. "The dinosaur season's off to a seriously lousy start this year. Terry's down with a stomach virus or something."

"Bet Brian's happy about that," said George. "They out at the trackway?"

"Brian is. Terry's here."

"How bad is he?"

"Bad enough. I want him to stay here today. If he's not better by tonight, I'm sending him home."

George's egg-laden fork paused halfway between his plate and his face. "How?"

Angstrom jerked a thumb at the van outside. "We can draw straws for the privilege."

"Well, I was hoping against hope." George gestured at Sally and himself with his fork, and the glob of egg slid off the tines and landed wetly beside his plate. "By *we*," he said to her, "he means *us*."

Sally made a small, plaintive sound. "I can't wait," she said, "until I, too, am a full-fledged scientist and don't get so many privileges."

Angstrom gave her a pitying smile as he stirred creamer into his coffee. "You won't lose but a few hours if you turn around and come straight back. And being full-fledged wouldn't make any difference in this case. Brian gets excited when he's got dino tracks in front of him. Couldn't haul him away with a team of oxen."

"Brian," George said around a mouthful of toast, "is basically excitable. Find anything interesting in Blanco County?"

Angstrom shook his head. "Some mosasaur teeth, and that's *all* we have to show for the time we spent there. This year the floods've covered up more of Blanco than they uncovered. Anyway, Brian was hot to get to the trackway. He went on out to the ranch, and I put Terry to bed."

"Brian can have his tracks," said George. "I want bones. I want my own dinosaur."

"Somewhere," Sally told him, "there must be one with your name on it."

"Well," Angstrom said, "we'll go on down to Big Bend day after tomorrow or the next day. Meanwhile, drink your water. Put some more salt on those eggs. It's going to be a hot, hot day, and with Terry laid up, Brian'll need your help."

George said, "Thrill," and drained his water glass. "When I was a kid, Mom and Dad always used to tell me to study hard in school or I'd be a ditch-digger all my life. So I studied real, real hard and grew up and decided to become a paleontologist. *Since* I became one, I figure I've moved about as much rock with my bare hands as there is in all of Brewster County, and sweated out enough salt to build my own life-sized model of Spindletop."

They ate in silence for a time. Then George pushed his plate away, leaned back in his chair, and folded his hands across his middle.

"We had a visitor at the lab day before yesterday," he said to Angstrom. "About half an hour after you three left, who should show up but our old buddy Polson."

Angstrom groaned. "Did he get *in?*"

"Walked right in."

Angstrom swore. "We've got some serious security problems at the lab."

"Sally and I were both in the back crating horses." George grinned. "He had a nice, long talk with Sally. At Sally, rather."

She looked sheepish. "Well, I didn't know who he was. I'm the new-hire, remember? George took one look at him and bolted."

It was George's turn to look sheepish. "Panicked. Sorry."

"You didn't let him near the specimens, I hope," Angstrom said. "You didn't let him see your maps."

"Well, he may have seen the maps," George said. "We had them spread all over the table in the front room, and there's no telling how long he was there before he wandered back to bother us."

Angstrom swore again. "That's just great. Now we'll probably have him underfoot all summer. Everywhere we go, there he'll be, driving God's own Winnebago."

Sally said, "God's own what?"

Angstrom looked at her. "Thought George would've told you about God's own Winnebago. Polson's got his own little mobile museum. He calls it God's own Winnebago. It's full of evidence, alleged, that people and dinosaurs co-existed, evolution's part of some great evil conspiracy, I don't know what all. He takes it out to Glen Rose and harangues the tourists as they go into the park to see the dino tracks. He's associated with crackpot groups all over Texas and Oklahoma."

"Well, he didn't get near our eohippi," Sally said. "I was standing between them and him the whole time."

"She was standing there with a nail-gun in her hand the whole time," said George. There was malicious glee in his chuckle. "Good thing for Polson it wasn't Brian. Brian would've stapled him to a wall and hung an exhibit card around his neck. Homo not so sapiens, extinct."

"Well, what did the man want this time?"

Sally said, "I sort of gathered he'd just got himself shown out of the Memorial Museum. He was all steamed up about conspiracy and the scientific establishment and stuff."

"As usual. How'd you get rid of him?"

"Used a strong grease-cutter!" George said, grinning and leaning forward. "No, get this, this is the best part. Here's this two-hundred-fifty-pound Pillsbury Doughboy in a bad suit, and *here's* our own little Sally, everybody's favorite hundred-twenty pounds of lady paleontologist—"

She looked at him indignantly. "One-twelve!"

"Right. One-twelve. Now. Sally listens to this sweaty madman rave for a full five minutes—"

"He sprayed me with spittle," she said, "he *breathed* on me," and horror was depicted in her countenance.

"—and then she looks him right in the face and tells him, 'Excuse me, your fly is open.' And he looks down and realizes that the whole time he's been standing there yelling and waving his arms in the air, he's had one tail of his shirt sticking out the front of his pants!"

Angstrom simply hung in his chair and howled laughter. "Oh, my heart," he gasped, patting himself on the chest, "Oh, my!" He wiped sway a tear. "Well done, Sally. I almost, *almost* feel sorry for the guy."

"Brian'll love it," said George.

"No kidding. Brian could learn from it, in fact. Couple of years ago, he almost booted some colleague of Polson's right out the door. I mean, tip of toe to seat of pants. What was that clown's name?"

"Letz," said George. "Lentz?"

"Lentschke. Came to the lab one day with a fish tooth or something he claimed he'd found lying inside one of the dino footprints at Glen Rose. I guess he thought it must've been lying there forever and we'd overlooked it or deliberately ignored it."

"Sure," George said, "it's not like stuff ever gets washed down the Palauxy River and deposited on the trackway, right?"

"Well," Angstrom went on, "Lentschke shoves this tooth or whatever into Brian's face and asks him if he knows what it is. Brian had no idea who this guy was, so he answers, perfectly seriously, 'Looks like a fish tooth to me, but I'm not sure. I'm an *ichn*ologist, you want an *ichth*yologist'. Lentschke asks him one more time, and

Brian tells him again, 'I'm just not sure, why don't you take it across the street to the fish lab?' So Lentschke leaves, and the next thing Brian knows, he's being quoted in this press release from the major crackpot-science group in Dallas, headline: top scientist baffled by mystery fossil! Two weeks later, Lentschke's back at the lab on some fresh errand of mischief, and Brian practically vaults over the bench to get at him. I had to grab him and hold him, and I mean, *hold* him. Brian's built like Tarzan. He'd've kicked Lentschke's butt to Waco."

"Should've let him," George said.

"Waco's too close to Austin," Sally said.

Angstrom looked at them reproachfully. "This was serious rage I'm talking about. We're lucky the next press release didn't say, Top Scientist Beats Man's Head In."

"Well, at least Brian seems to've made his point," George said. "The guy's never been back to the lab."

A county sheriff's office car pulled into the motel parking lot and drew up alongside the van. A thin sheriff's deputy wearing mirror sunglasses got out. He started toward the manager's office, locked looks with Angstrom through the window of the coffee shop, and came inside and straight over to the paleontologists' table.

"'Scuse me," the deputy said, "you the folks who's with a Brian Barbee?"

"Why, yes."

"Better come with me down to the county courthouse."

"Oh, no," George said. "Brian's gone and punched somebody out."

The deputy's head swiveled toward him. The big reflective lenses and the pinched mouth made Angstrom think of praying mantises. "Your Brian Barbee's *dead*."

Sheriff Boyd Daigle let his bloodshot eyes flicker briefly over George and Sally, and it was obvious to Angstrom that the man disapproved of the one graduate student's beard and the other's very presence. Daigle was about sixty years old, a big, knobby, sunburned man with a face like a dried apple. The main elements of decor in his office at the county courthouse were gunracks, stuffed birds, and deer antlers. He said, "Thought there was one more of you."

"My other grad student's back at the motel," Angstrom said. "He's got a stomach virus. I left a message for him, if he wakes up." He looked down at his own strong, leather-skinned hands. They seemed about half the size of the sheriff's. "What happened to Brian?"

The sheriff turned slightly in his swivel chair and nodded toward Sally. "Sure you want her to hear this?"

"Don't stop on my account," Angstrom heard her say. He looked around at her. She was as pale as chalk.

"Suit yourself, Miss Hoffman."

"Hofner," she said.

"Suit yourself, Miss Hofner." Daigle transferred his attention back to Angstrom. "We got the body back just a little while ago and ain't had time to do the autopsy yet. But it pretty much looks like somebody hit your Professor Barbee smack between the eyes with a blunt instrument. Dropped him like a poleaxed cow."

Angstrom shivered. One of the graduate students sitting behind him groaned. He had no idea whether it was Sally or George. He swallowed hard and said, "Do you know who did it?"

"Well, we're working on finding out who."

Angstrom could think of nothing to say except, "Are you *sure* it's Brian?"

"Ray," Daigle said to a deputy who had been standing next to a file cabinet near the door. Ray was an onion-shaped man with an unholstered pistol stuck into the waistband of his trousers. A convenient bulge of fat held the gun securely in place. He picked a large manila envelope off the top of the file cabinet and brought it over to the sheriff. Daigle undid the clasp with a flick of a thumbnail as big around as a quarter and emptied the contents onto his desk blotter. There was a thick, sealed business envelope with $127.43 cash, $450 travel checks, visa, chevron, diam. shamrock and initials scrawled on it. There were two ballpoint pens, a wristwatch, a key ring with six keys on it, a pocket-sized notebook, and a worn brown leather wallet. Daigle scooped up the wallet in his catcher's-mitt-sized hand and flipped it open to the driver's license. He held it up so that Angstrom could see the picture on the license.

"I'm real sure, Professor Angstrom." He closed the wallet and put it down. "This is all the loose stuff your friend had on him. There's also a knapsack, toolbelt, and a U.T. van full of camping gear and things. The van's still out to the Ullrich ranch." He picked up the envelope containing the money. "All you scientists this well-heeled?"

"It's the start of dinosaur season," Angstrom said. "The field season. Brian and Terry—that's Terry Sharp, my sick grad student at the motel—Brian and Terry were planning to spend most of the summer camped out at the Ullrich ranch. That money would've had to last them. Food and gas, mainly. A beer every now and then."

"Would of had to be beer. Ain't nothing else in the whole county."

"Brian's—Brian wasn't much of a drinker."

"I'm sure it's just as well." The sheriff shoveled everything back into the manila envelope and returned it to Deputy Ray. "Big man drinks a lot, he's liable to be a handful for somebody. Now, near as the M.E. can tell, your friend was killed sometime late yesterday afternoon. Duane Ullrich's boy, Ron, found him around dawn this morning. Ron was going fishing under the bridge down from where the dinosaur footprints is. Suppose you help me fit all this into a time frame."

Angstrom said, "Brian and Terry and I left Austin on Tuesday. We spent the afternoon and the next morning looking around at several sites in Blanco County and camped out at one of them. We got here about three yesterday. Terry was starting to feel pretty bad by then, so I checked him into the motel with me. Brian took the van out to the ranch. The last time I saw him was just a little before four, in the parking lot."

"Duane Ullrich says your friend come by the ranch about half past to say hello." Daigle indicated Sally and George with a nod. "What about these two?"

"They had an exhibit of horse fossils to finish for the Nature Center Annex in Austin. They weren't able to leave town until early this morning. The original plan was for the three of us, George and Sally and me, to go on to Big Bend this weekend. Big Bend's usually where we spend most of the season."

"I been to Big Bend." Daigle looked past Angstrom, at, it seemed to him, Sally. "Park or no, it ain't the sort of place I'd pick for summer vacation." The bloodshot gaze returned to Angstrom. "Duane had his boy show Professor Barbee down to the creek, and then Ron walked back. It's about a mile from the house to as close to the creek as you can get a vehicle in, unless you want to go all the way around and use the old county road. Runs behind the Ullrich property and brings you right to the old bridge. From where the van's parked to where the footprints is is about another half a mile. Now, the plan was for all five of you to camp out there?"

"Everyone except me," said Angstrom. "I usually get a motel room if there's one close enough."

"How come?"

"It's the privilege of emeriti."

The sheriff blinked. "Of who?"

"Emeriti. Plural of emeritus." Angstrom gave the sheriff a wan smile. "Meaning, old buzzards like me." Daigle did not respond to the smile, and Angstrom felt it go away. "Can we go out to the trackway, Sheriff?"

"I guess you have to. I guess the University of Texas will want its van back. But I better take you. We been over the area once already, but I don't want it disturbed until we been over it again, real good."

"I know how not to disturb an area."

"Well, that's good. Maybe while we're out there, you can explain to me how Professor Barbee'd let somebody just walk up and hit him between the eyes."

Everyone in Sheriff Daigle's office was silent for a long moment. Finally, Angstrom turned in his chair, and to George and Sally he said, "I think you'd better go back to the motel and stay with Terry."

The two graduate students exchanged glances, and Sally said, "Meaning, I should go back?"

"This is going to be unpleasant."

"It's already unpleasant. It's already gone a long way past unpleasant. I've—I want to go with you."

"Look," said George, "*I'll* go babysit Terry." He looked almost hopefully at Angstrom. "Did you tell Terry in your note—about Brian?"

Angstrom shook his head. "I was hoping this'd all turn out to be a mistake."

"Guess you want me to tell him, huh?"

"Use your own judgment." Angstrom handed him the room key. "Do what you think is best. Only don't wake him up just to tell him. If he's asleep, let him go on sleeping."

"Right. Well." George puffed out his bearded cheeks and exhaled with a soft hiss. "Guess I'll see you back at the motel," he said. He turned, and was gone.

Sheriff Daigle gave Sally an unhappy look. "We've moved the body, but there's lots of blood out there. Sure you want to do this?"

"Either order me to go back with George, or catch up with the times. I *want* to do this." She waited for either Angstrom or the sheriff to reply, and then, when neither of them did, she said, "Fine. I need a restroom."

"End of the hall," said Deputy Ray, "door on the right." She left.

Daigle said, "She got something to prove?"

"She's still hacked off about Antarctica."

The sheriff raised eyebrows that were like tufts of steel wool. "Don't get you."

"A couple of years back, the professor she'd been working with at Texas Tech decided to go look for fossils in Antarctica. He refused to take her along. Said Antarctica was no place for a woman."

"From what I hear, it ain't." The sheriff looked thoughtful for a moment. "She know Professor Barbee very well?"

"Of course. They've been working together at the Austin lab for almost two years."

"I mean, did she know him really well?"

"Ah. No. I don't think so. Brian has a girlfriend. Had a—oh, God, I forgot all about Larraine." He looked at the sheriff almost pleadingly. "I'd better give her a call."

"Let it wait a little while."

"Sheriff, who do you think could've killed Brian?"

"Well, he just might of run into trouble with transients." Daigle swiveled behind his desk and gestured at a large county map framed in glass on the wall. "I spend a goodly amount of time driving people to the county line and letting 'em off. This is a, what you call a hunger county. There's not many jobs here, and the ones there is is taken. So I just tell people moving through to keep right on moving. Mostly it's younger people. Sometimes it's families with children and if that don't break your heart. But sometimes it's somebody who's just plain bad news."

The sheriff's chair squeaked a protest as he reached for a yardstick. He raised an amazing length of arm, and there was a small, hard click as the tip of the yardstick tapped against the glass.

"That there's the Ullrich ranch," he said. "And that—" click "— is the creek and the old county road. Folks like Duane, living out a ways from town, keep a loaded shotgun handy. For rattlesnakes and other troublemakers. But I don't think a transient killed your friend. Ain't no sign of a camp, for one thing. For two, hundred and twenty-some-odd dollars is a lot of money to pass up. Plus, they'd of taken everything else he had on him."

"Then who else could've done it?"

The tufted steel-wool eyebrows met over the bridge of Daigle's nose. "There's people who's involved in drugs."

"Drugs?" Sally said. "Serious, heavy drugs, out *here?*"

She and Angstrom were in the back seat of a county sheriff's office car. The thin deputy with the mirror sunglasses was driving. Sheriff Daigle seemed to fill half of the cabin. He looked back at her and smiled sardonically.

"This is one of our slow weeks," he said. "Last month, we caught two brothers running a speed lab in their barn. They still report stuff like that in Austin?"

"They love to report stuff like that in Austin," Angstrom said.

Daigle nodded. "Good. I hate to think in the big city everybody thinks we got our thumbs up our behinds here. 'Scuse my language, Miss. Out here, you got your people raising marijuana and running it all over the southwest. You got 'em keeping open the lines of communication for the big-city family businesses, if you know what

I mean. The ones that's been involved in some bad crap or other ever since Prohibition days. 'Scuse me. The central Texas drug pipeline runs right through this county. I got Texas Rangers and federal agents out here nearly all the time. There's parts of this county that's as bad as the old Jacksboro Highway up around Fort Worth ever was. I lost a good deputy over to Molley last summer. He pulled over this suspicious truck, and the driver shot him in the chest with a nine mil. My deputy put a forty-four magnum slug through the truck door as he was falling over backwards. Blew the driver all over the inside of the cab."

As Daigle related this, it again seemed to Angstrom that he was studying Sally's face, trying to gauge her reaction. She appeared unimpressed with the sheriff's tales. She looked as tired and irritable as Angstrom felt.

"They report stuff like that back in Austin, too?" said Daigle.

Angstrom repressed a frown. "We were at Big Bend last summer and didn't get the papers. What's this have to do with Brian?"

"Ever' so often," Daigle said, "somebody from Austin or someplace decides to go off hiking or camping in these hills. I guess they stumble into one of the local grower's marijuana fields or see something else they ain't supposed to see. After a bit, somebody back in Austin gets to missing 'em, and I got to go take a look. And never find a thing. If you know a nice, private place where you can plant a whole field of marijuana, you're sure going to know places to stash bodies so they ain't never found. I think your friend just showed up at the wrong place at the wrong time."

Angstrom looked out his window as the deputy swung the car off the main highway, onto a two-lane blacktop. Most of what he actually knew about organized crime and drug-trafficking had been haphazardly gleaned over the years from television news programs and the opening paragraphs of newspaper stories, and it had become thoroughly mixed with images acquired in equally haphazard fashion from movies. He thought of organized criminals, if that was what one called them, as lupine men and occasionally simian men who wore dark shirts, light ties, and sharkskin suits. He could not imagine such men consorting with cowboy-hatted, cowboy-booted Bubba out on the ranch, stepping carefully around cowflops so as not to ruin their expensive shoes.

"Over there's the Ullrich place," Daigle said as the car passed a modest but well-tended house and outbuildings. "We'll stop and have a chit-chat with Duane on the way back. Up here's the turnoff to the creek."

Angstrom said, "Is Duane Ullrich one of your local growers?"

The sheriff glowered at him, glanced ahead as the car slowed, left the blacktop, and began crunching over gravel, and then looked back at him with the glower still in place.

"Duane Ullrich and me," Daigle said, "has been friends all our lives. He's got no more use'n me for drugs or people who's involved in drugs. His boy Ron's okay, too. Now, if Duane *was* growing marijuana on his property, he sure wouldn't invite a bunch of nosey sci'ntists to come walk all over the place. Duane guesses these footprints on his land is probably as good as the Glen Rose ones. He guesses he'll get on television. Think so?"

"It could happen."

"Well, there you are." The sheriff smiled with satisfaction. "If you're involved in drugs, television *ain't* the kind of attention you want to attract."

The car reached the end of the graveltop. The other University of Texas van and another county sheriff's office car were parked on the pebble-carpeted rim of a long, rocky slope. At the bottom of the slope, trees marked the course of the creek. Two deputies stood waiting. The sheriff told his passengers to remain in the car for a minute, and both he and the thin deputy got out and walked over. The four lawmen talked and gesticulated. Angstrom looked at Sally. She sat grim-faced, staring out the window in the direction of the creek. He left her alone.

Daigle and his thin deputy returned. The sheriff opened the rear door on Sally's side and said, "Let's go on down to the creek." The thin deputy opened Angstrom's door for him, then leaned in through the driver's door and came back out holding a pump-action shotgun. He saw the questioning look on the scientist's face and said "Rattlesnakes." It was the first thing Angstrom could remember hearing him say since breakfast. Breakfast seemed a hundred million years ago.

"Let's reconstruct this," the sheriff said as he and the two paleontologists and the thin deputy moved around to the front of the van.

"Professor Barbee parks and gets out. I guess he's real eager, 'cause he just grabs his knapsack and his toolbelt and heads for the creek."

"He wouldn't've been able to think about anything else," Angstrom said. "He was very excited about this trackway."

Daigle pointed downstream. "There's the old bridge. Rickety old iron frame with wood planks laid crossways. Been standing longer than I have. Shakes and rattles in a medium breeze, and, ever' spring, I keep expecting it to wash away. Me, I wouldn't want to ride a bicycle across. But drug-runners is always barreling around on these old roads. I think your friend may of seen something illegal, maybe at the bridge. We found a place on the left bank where somebody slid down and then later climbed back up. One person, near as we can tell."

"Why would drug-traffickers just leave Brian lying there?" said Angstrom. "I thought you said the idea was to *not* draw attention to a place."

Daigle shrugged. "Professor Barbee must of weighed, what, two hundred pounds? Mostly solid pounds, too. It's my experience a body always seems to weigh four times more dead than when it was alive. Maybe whoever killed him was in a hurry. Maybe it was hot like now, and they looked at how big he was and said, 'Forget it'."

They walked in file through sparse, calf high grass, past slabs of rock like petrified mattresses, the deputy leading, the sheriff bringing up the rear. They passed through the trees, crossed the floodline, and went down a steep bank of dry, hard clay, onto a gravel bar. Beyond a narrow ribbon of virtually motionless green water was a long, low table of limestone. The limestone bore scores of impressions of three-toed, claw-tipped feet, some of them with spreads of eighteen inches. Angstrom drew a sharp breath, and for just a moment Brian was forgotten, heat, weariness, age, and everything else were forgotten, as a rapturous awe filled him.

They were right here, he thought. Eighty, eighty-five million years ago, they passed not fifty feet from where I'm standing—and he could see them as they passed—forearms tucked daintily against deep chests, great, tooth-filled heads and long, stiff tails held high as they walked, churning up the limy mud with those gargantuan chicken feet of theirs, masters of a world in which Homo sapiens existed not even as a gleam in some ratty little insectivore's eye.

The moment passed, and Angstrom murmured, "Carnosaurs."

"Beg pardon?" said the sheriff.

"A whole pack of carnosaurs." He saw the blank look on the lawman's face. "The big meat-eating dinosaurs. Tyrannosaurus and its lesser cousins."

Daigle seemed almost impressed. "We had T'rannosaurus around here?"

"Probably Acrocanthosaurus. One of the lesser cousins, but still a nasty piece of work."

The sheriff spat to one side. "Guess we're real lucky they're all gone, then. Reverend Bradshaw says they all drowned in Noah's flood."

Angstrom regarded him levelly and said, "What do you say, Sheriff?"

Daigle matched his look. "I know you people think the world's billions of years old and we all come up from lower animals. I believe in the revealed word of God. If it says everything was made in six twenty-four-hour days, that's good enough for me."

"I'm not attacking your faith, Sheriff."

The sheriff shrugged and gazed at the trackway. "I got nothing against your dinosaurs, either. I saw the bones of some in a museum over to San Antonio last year. My grandson wanted to go. He loves dinosaurs. He was real impressed with the one with all the horns. And he asked me why Noah'd let a big, wonderful thing like that drown but save a lot of nasty little fire ants and scorpions."

"What did you tell him?"

"I said to him, 'Danged if I know'." They stepped easily across the sunken creek, and then Daigle gestured at the ground. "About here's where Professor Barbee dropped his knapsack and toolbelt."

He pointed toward the far end of the limestone bar. "Down there's where he was killed."

Angstrom looked downstream. He frowned and said, "Why'd Brian drop the knapsack and toolbelt here?"

"You're the pee-aitch-dee," Sheriff Daigle said. "You tell me."

They walked carefully across the ancient churned-up surface. At the end of the limestone slab, the sheriff said, unnecessarily, "Here's where Professor Barbee was killed," and, just as unnecessarily, pointed to a large reddish-brown stain on the rock. Metallic-green flies buzzed about the stain and kept alighting on it. Angstrom saw Sally turn her face quickly and saw Daigle give his deputy a told-her-so look.

"Now," the sheriff said, "here's the part nobody understands. Here's your friend digging at this end of the tracks, and he's got a clear view of about a half a mile, from past where he come down the slope to past the bridge. And somebody still walks right up and knocks him in the head."

Angstrom squatted beside the bloodstain and tried to wave the flies away. They easily avoided his hand and went on about their business. "The part I still don't get is, if Brian was here, what was his equipment doing back there on the gravel bar?"

"It's hot out on this rock. Maybe he didn't want to lug around a bunch of stuff in the heat."

"Then what was Brian digging *with?*"

"Whatever you use to dig with, I guess."

"Sheriff, these tracks are still full of sand and grit from last month's floods. Brian never touched them."

Daigle opened his mouth to say something, thought better of it, closed his mouth. He glared around at the ground for a second, then pointed triumphantly at a spot several feet away. "I ain't *entirely* stupid," he growled. "That's fresh-chipped rock there."

Angstrom moved crabwise to the place and ran his hand over it. He motioned to Sally, and she knelt beside him. The two law men hesitated for a moment before bending down to peer at the patch of rock between the paleontologists. The sheriff said, "What is it?"

Angstrom gave him a grim look. "I think it's what got Brian Barbee killed."

Daigle peered some more. "So what *is* it?"

"What does it look like?"

The sheriff did not answer immediately. His face slowly folded itself into a complex system of ridges and furrows. At last he said, "A footprint. A real old petrified human footprint."

"Wrong on all counts," Angstrom said. "It's not real, it's no older than yesterday, and it's not a footprint, human or otherwise. The depression that looks sort of like the bottom of a foot is just a shallow basin made by erosion. There's none of the squishing that occurs when an object's pushed down into mud and then pulled out. The toe marks were carved by the same person who killed Brian."

The lawmen stepped back as the paleontologists stood up. Daigle's expression was skeptical. The deputy gnawed the inside of a cheek for a second, then said, "There's human footprints mixed in with the dinosaur ones up at Glen Rose."

"I've seen them," said Angstrom. "They're fakes, too, the work of someone in the so-called creation-science movement."

The deputy's knuckles began to whiten on the shotgun. "Reverend Bradshaw from our church went up and seen 'em, too. He *preached* about 'em. They ain't no more fakes than these."

"It's unweathered, fresh-chipped rock, Frank," Daigle said to the deputy, very gently. "Even I can see that." He looked unhappy as he turned back to Angstrom and sounded unhappy when he spoke. "You're saying somebody killed your friend and then carved these toe marks."

"It was probably the other way around."

"Professor Angstrom," said the sheriff, "I know a lot of fine people who hate your evolution theories even more'n I do. Ain't one of 'em's ever struck me as being the least bit murderous."

Angstrom looked the big lawman right in the eye and said, "Like I said, I'm not attacking faith here, just bad science. But you of all people should know that anybody who gets mad enough or scared enough can kill. Brian could be plenty scary. He was a strong, very physical man, something of a hothead, too. He despised the creation-science movement with what I can only describe as crusading fervor. He was an ichnologist. That's a paleontologist whose specialty is fossil footprints, only in his case, it was more, it was his passion. He was excited about this trackway. He'd've regarded these carvings as a desecration, just like he regarded the ones at Glen Rose. I think when he came down the bank and through the trees back there, he saw someone chipping at the rock here and knew immediately what was going on. I think he shed his equipment and came charging over like a mad bull. Probably he was screaming bloody murder. I think he'd've done some serious pushing and shoving when he got hold of whoever was here."

"And whoever was here," said Daigle, "just hauled off and hit him with a hammer or chisel and then run off in a panic." He nodded toward the bridge. "Run off that way, same way as he come in, so he must of had a car or something parked up there. Duane said the only person who come by yesterday was Professor Barbee. But if the person who made these marks didn't come expecting to be attacked by your friend, why'd he go to all the bother of using that old back road?"

"So the toe marks would *be here*." Angstrom made a gesture that took in the whole trackway. "A spectacular site like this is going to draw a fair amount of media attention. I'm sure the idea was for somebody to show up at about the time the television coverage was heaviest, point to the supposed human footprint, say, 'Look what the scientific establishment can't deny but won't acknowledge.'"

"I guess it'd hurt your case some, huh?"

Angstrom shook his head emphatically. "Not in the least. Any reputable scientist would take one look at this alleged footprint and know it's a fake. Creation science is long on this kind of thing because it's short on everything else. Nothing its proponents could do to this site in an excess of zeal would hurt our case or help theirs."

"The maps," said Sally, quietly. Angstrom and the sheriff turned to stare at her.

"We had all our maps out in the front room," she said, "where anybody who walked into the lab could've seen them. If he wanted to get even for what happened and strike a blow for the cause at the same time—"

"Oh, *no!*" Angstrom cried out. "Not *him!*"

"—all he had to do, if there's anyone here who's in the movement, was pick up the phone and get directions."

"Polson!" Angstrom shrieked. "*Polson!*"

Daigle scowled. "Now who's Polson?"

Angstrom beat his fist against the eighty-million-year-old rock. "Look for a man making a getaway in God's own Winnebago."

Upstart

You must obey the edict of the Sreen," the Intermediaries have told us repeatedly, "there is no appeal," but the captain won't hear of it, not for a moment. He draws himself up to his full height of two meters and looms threateningly over the four or five Intermediaries, who are, after all, small and not particularly substantial-looking beings, mere wisps of translucent flesh through which their bluish skeletal structures and pulsing organs can be seen.

"You take us in to talk to the Sreen," the captain tells them, "you take us in right *now*, do you hear me?" His voice is like a sword coming out of its scabbard, an angry, menacing, deadly metal-on-metal rasp. "You take us to these God-damned Sreen of yours and let us talk to them."

The Intermediaries shrink before him, fluttering their pallid appendages in obvious dismay, and bleat in unison, "No, no, what you request is impossible. The decision of the Sreen is final, and, anyway, they're very busy right now, they can't be bothered."

The captain wheels savagely, face mottled, teeth bared, arms windmilling with rage. I have never seen him this furious before, and it frightens me. Not that I cannot appreciate and even share his anger toward the Sreen, of course. The Sreen have been very arbitrary and high-handed from the start, snatching our vessel out of normal space, scooping it up and stuffing it into the maw of their own craft, establishing communication with us through their Intermediaries, then issuing their incredible edict. They do not appear to care that they have interfered with Humankind's grandest endeavor. Our vessel is Terra's first bona fide starship, in which the captain and I were to have accelerated through normal space to light-velocity, activated the tardyon-tachyon conversion system and popped back into normal space in the neighborhood of Alpha Centauri. I can understand how the captain feels.

At the same time, I'm afraid that his rage will get us into extremely serious trouble. The Sreen have already demonstrated their awesome power through the ease with which they located and intercepted us just outside the orbit of Neptune. Their vessel is incomprehensible, a drupelet-cluster of a construct which seems to move in casual defiance of every law of physics, half in normal space, half in elsewherespace. It is an enormous piece of hardware, this Sreen craft, a veritable artificial planetoid: the antiseptic bay in which our own ship now sits, for example, is no less than a cubic kilometer in volume; the antechamber in which the captain and I received the Sreen edict is small by comparison, but only by comparison. Before us is a great door of dully gleaming gray metal, five or six meters high, approximately four wide. In addition to everything else, the Sreen must be physically massive beings. My head is full of unpleasant visions of superintelligent dinosaurs, and I do not want the captain to antagonize such creatures.

"Sir," I say "there's nothing we can do here. We're just going to have to return home and let Earth figure a way out of this thing. Let them handle it." Absurd, absurd, I know how absurd the suggestion is even as I voice it, no one on Earth is going to be able to defy the edict. "We haven't any choice, sir, they want us to go now, and I think we'd better do it."

The captain glares at me and balls his meaty hands into fists. I tense in expectation of blows which do not fall. Instead, he shakes his head emphatically and turns to the Intermediaries. "This is ridiculous. Thoroughly ridiculous."

"Captain—"

He silences me with an imperious gesture. "Who do the Sreen think they *are*?"

"The true and indisputable masters of the universe," the Intermediaries pipe in one high but full-toned voice, "the lords of Creation."

"I want to see them," the captain insists.

"You must return to your ship," they insist, "and obey the will of the Sreen."

"Like hell! Like bloody God-damned hell! Where are they? What makes them think they have the right, the *right*, to claim the whole damned *universe* for themselves?" The captain's voice is going up the scale, becoming a shriek, and filled though I am with terror of the Sreen, I am also caught up in fierce admiration for my superior officer. He may be a suicidal fool to refuse to accept the situation, but there is passion in his foolishness, and it is an infectious passion. "How *dare* they treat us this way? What do they *mean*, ordering us to go home and stay there because *they* own the universe?"

He takes a step toward the door. The Intermediaries move to block his path. With an inarticulate screech, he ploughs through them, swatting them aside with the backs of his hands, kicking them out of his way with his heavy-booted feet. The Intermediaries break easily, and it occurs to me then that they are probably as disposable a commodity among the Sreen as tissue paper is among human beings. One Intermediary is left limping along after the captain. Through the clear pale skin of its back, I see that some vertebrae have been badly dislocated. The thing nevertheless succeeds in overtaking the captain and wrapping its appendages around his calf, bleating all the while, "No, no, you must abide by the edict, even as every other inferior species has, you must abide..." The captain is having trouble disentangling himself, and so I go to him. Together, we tear the Intermediary loose. The captain flings it aside, and it bounces off the great portal, spins across the polished floor, lies crushed and unmoving.

Side by side, we pause directly before the door. My teeth, I suddenly realize, are chattering with fear. "Captain," I say as my resolve begins to disintegrate, "why are we doing this?"

"The nature of the beast," he mutters, almost sadly, and smacks the palm of his gloved hand against the portal. "Sreen!" he yells. "Come out, Sreen!"

And we wait.

"If we don't make it home from this," I say at length, "if they never hear from us back on Earth, never know what became of their starship—"

"They'll just keep tossing men and women at the stars until someone does come back. Sreen or no Sreen." The captain strikes the door again, with the edge of his fist this time. "Sreen!" A bellow which, curiously, does not echo in the vast antechamber. "*Sreen!* SREEN!"

The door starts to swing back on noiseless hinges, and a breath of cold, unbelievably cold air touches our faces. The door swings open. The door swings open. The door swings open forever before we finally see into the next chamber.

"Oh my God," I whisper to the captain, "oh, oh my God."

They are titans, they are the true and indisputable masters of the universe, the lords of Creation, and they are unhappy with us. They speak, and theirs is a voice that shatters mountains.

"WHO. ARE. YOU?"

The captain's lips draw back over his teeth in a mirthless grin as he plants his fists on his hips, throws back his head, thrusts out his jaw. "Who wants to know?"

Two Women of the Prairie

It never occurred to her to complain. Things were the way they were. When her daughter died, her son-in-law's familial obligations ended, and he was free to seek another wife. She was free to choose between getting by as well as she could for as long as she could, with no living relatives to help her and in the face of the fact that no one who was not a relative owed her a thing, or else staying behind and waiting to die when the band moved on.

Her will to live proved stronger than her pride. She became a scavenger, subsisting on others' garbage. She had no lodge skins or poles, and no animals to haul them if she had; she fashioned for herself a rude shelter of rags and sticks, which she carried in a bundle on her back when the band traveled.

Old woman! old woman! the children might call, and make faces, and dash away laughing, delighted at their own cleverness. No one else paid any attention to her unless it was strictly necessary.

Get out of the way, old woman, a man might say as he came by on his pony — unless, of course, the man happened to be her former son-in-law, in which case he would ignore her as steadfastly as he had from the moment of his marriage to her daughter. It was considered bad form to speak to one's mother-in-law, worse if she were dead, too. She bore being dead, being ignored, being insulted, as she bore everything else, with a scavenger's patience.

It was only late at night, as she lay in her miserable shelter, that she sometimes permitted herself to dwell upon the series of calamities that had befallen her. She would stroke one mutilated hand with the other and count the missing finger knuckles, each lopped off in token of mourning for a dead relative. Husband, brothers, sons, daughter. She would recall what it had been to have ten fully functioning fingers, and then what it had been to be young, smooth-skinned, pretty. She had been all of those things. More than one young man, affecting nonchalance as he passed playing his flute, had singled her out in a group of marriageable maidens and tried to flirt with her, only to have his composure wrecked by girlish taunts and laughter. One man had finally paid her father many horses for her; no one could have been more impressed by her value than she herself was.

Late one night, as she thought about those horses, the will to live finally did gutter in her, like a flame in a draft. She crawled out of her shelter and walked away from the sleeping camp.

She walked in no particular direction and never bothered to look back, for she knew that no one behind her cared. She walked with the wind, and it urged her on her way. She walked for hours, strangely tireless, as though she had saved up strength over the years for this very occasion. The stars passed overhead, the moon fell slowly, the eastern sky lightened. At last the hours and the miles told on her. She was stiff and in pain, and the chill had settled through her withered flesh, into her bones. She was thirsty and hungry, too. Still, it never occurred to her to complain.

In the dream, if it was a dream, if she had actually been asleep in bed and dreaming and not lying awake in bed and thinking, the prairie spread away from Rebecca to a circle of horizon. She was the only thing moving in that grassy expanse. She was moving at a dead run, clawing at the air with her hands as though she could grab it and pull it past and increase her speed by that much. She had shed her clothes, and her loosened hair streamed behind her. Her eyes were wide. She had her mouth open, screaming. She looked like a madwoman.

She started, and the vision vanished. Embers glowed in the hearth, casting barely enough light upon the sod hut's walls and ceiling to show her they were there. So I have been dreaming, she thought, and turned on her half of the rough bed toward her husband's vacant half. Not seeing him there had begun to seem normal. It had been strange at first, as strange as seeing him there had been after the wedding. One adjusted, so that each strange new thing became a familiar old thing. Six weeks earlier, she had watched her husband ride off on the one horse, leading the one mule, and heard him promise to return within a fortnight. Since then, she had felt herself tugged in several directions at once by the hope that he still would come back, the fear, now passed into expectation, that he might not, ever, and the deepening suspicion that he had never intended to do so. He had taken the one firearm and most of the tools.

She rose from the bed and moved to the window. There was no glass, only a greasy cloth covering; she drew it back and looked hatefully out at the prairie. Dark clouds lay low on the horizon, and the air was cool and heavy with moisture.

As she had done every morning since her husband's departure, she took inventory of foodstuffs: so much corn meal left, so much coffee, syrup, beans. She needed fresh water. She shouldered the yoke with the bucket suspended from either end and trudged toward the creek bottom, half a mile away. Near the low mound of the sod hut, the path took her by a narrow circular pit. Dirt lay in a heap next to the pit, and a shovel had been left stuck blade-deep into the heap. You were a brute and a wretched rascal, she told her absent husband, but the least you might have done was get that well dug before you up and rode off.

Then she told herself, as she had told herself many times during the past six weeks, I need to bring that shovel inside.

The storm was coming fast. Something else, coming more slowly, caught her eye as she returned from the creek bed. She took the water buckets in to that part of the room which she reserved as the kitchen, then stepped back outside.

A speck moved on the prairie. She watched it for a full minute before recognizing it as a person, and then her first thought was that it was her husband. That whoever was coming was coming on foot did not register at once. She took one more step away from the door, stood almost perfectly motionless, and watched for a very longtime. No, not her husband, but, still, a person, someone, another human being. Yes, it was. Yes. She had not seen a human being other than her husband in seven months. Lord God in Heaven, yes.

She waved and hallooed. The wind seemed to snatch the sound right out of her mouth, and when she started to run, waving both arms, it resisted her solidly. Forty yards from the hut, she had to stop. Bent forward, hands on knees, panting, she squinted against the wind, trying to see.

And at last she saw that it was a woman, an old woman, an old Indian woman at that, thin, dirty, tired-looking. The old woman came within yards of Rebecca before appearing to notice her. Then she stopped abruptly, drew a frayed, filthy blanket more tightly about her shoulders, and just looked at her. Rebecca had no idea of what to expect. She had seen few Indians since coming here, and those few had been distant figures on horseback, keeping their distance, going well around the homestead.

Lightning flashed on the horizon, and thunder rolled across the prairie. Black clouds were approaching very fast. Rebecca cleared her throat nervously and said, "You had better get back to where you belong." She pointed at the advancing clouds. "There's a bad storm coming."

The old woman's blanket slipped off one shoulder, exposing a ragged dress, but still she did not move, speak, or look away.

"Best you find some shelter for yourself," Rebecca said, taking a step away. The old woman did not move. The black clouds did.

The light faded as quickly and definitely as though a mourning veil had been drawn across the world, and Rebecca was suddenly very cold. An icy bead of rain struck her with stinging force just below her left eye. She took five more steps in the direction of the hut and stopped to look back. The old woman swayed slightly, took a single step after her, and then the wind bent her over until she was on her hands and knees.

Rebecca hesitated, ran back to her, leaned over her. She was staring at the patch of ground framed by her hands, moaning — or chanting, Rebecca could not tell which. The old woman looked up only when Rebecca said, in exasperation, "Then come on!" and made a frantic gesture for her to follow. "Come on, come on! Into the soddy!"

Curiosity, or perhaps it was only perplexity, suffused the seamed dark face. Encouraged, Rebecca grabbed one greasy sleeve of her dress and tugged her to her feet. She weighed less than her blanket. She weighed nothing at all. The wind seemed to propel them across the ground to the hut. The old woman balked at the door, but she was small and weak; Rebecca, of big-boned European stock, practically carried her in under her arm and deposited her by the hearth. Hail struck the door like a musket volley as she closed it.

She secured the cloth over the window to keep out the draft, then moved to the center of the room and from there to the back wall and around until she arrived at the hearth, opposite her guest.

Neither she nor the old woman took eyes off each other as she made the circuit.

What have I done? Rebecca asked herself, but she knew. She said, "I could not leave you out there to die."

It required a major effort of will to look away long enough to determine the state of the fire. She took some dried dung from the pile on her side of the hearth and pushed it into the flames. The old women sat on the dirt floor with her knees drawn up under her chin. Her bare feet were so dirty they were black. She relaxed by degrees, settled in place, rested her head and shoulder against the wall, but stayed watchful. Finally, because Rebecca did not know what else to do, she made coffee. "I guess you would like some breakfast," she said, "and I guess I have to give it to you." She realized that she would have to turn her back on the old woman to take the two tin cups off their pegs, sticks her husband had driven into the wall at shoulder height. The nape of her neck tingled as she did it.

The old woman was plainly startled when offered a cup of hot black liquid. She would not accept the cup, though the aromatic steam from it obviously interested her. Rebecca carefully set the cup on the floor before her and drew back.

"I guess you do not know about coffee," she said. Or was it the cup? Did Indians drink like beasts?

She set her three-legged skillet on the fire to heat and mixed up some corncakes. The old woman's nostrils twitched as they cooked. Rebecca became aware of another smell in the close atmosphere of the hut. She was no stranger to stench, but she felt herself overwhelmed by the other's commingled odor of unwashed body, rancid grease, and the Lord only knew what else. She poured a little water into a metal basin and got a brush and a precious bit of soap. She set these before the old woman, who regarded them incuriously and then watched Rebecca roll up her sleeves.

"You have to wash," Rebecca said, "if you expect to stay inside." She made a scrubbing motion along her own forearm. "Wash." She reached over and touched the back of the old woman's hand. The old woman did not seem to mind. She did not seem to care. Rebecca slid her fingers under the palm, gently took grip, and drew the hand toward herself. It was then that she saw the nubs of bone protruding from the truncated fingers. She recoiled with a little cry. "What happened to you?"

The question went unanswered, unacknowledged. Rebecca made herself reach for the hand again. The old woman let her take it. Rebecca said, "We'll tend to it in a minute," splashed a little water on the hand, and carefully soaped it. She tried not to touch the bony stubs or to think about them. She used the brush gently, as if she were bathing a baby —

Not here, not his ....

She clamped her teeth together and went on with her scrubbing. The old woman suffered first the hand to be washed, then part of the wrist, then the other hand. Rebecca sat back on her haunches, unsure how to proceed. Well, she told herself, it's a beginning, and set the brush and the basin aside for the time being.

When the corncakes were cooked, she put half of them on a plate, poured on a little sweet syrup, and set the plate on the floor before the old woman, next to the untouched cup of coffee. She took her own food at the rickety table. The old woman ate ravenously, licked crumbs off the sticky plate, tried to pick up a particle of bread that had fallen on the floor. It resisted her best efforts to grab it between thumb and forefinger. At last she moistened a bony stub with her tongue, daubed at the crumb and got it, and —

Rebecca quickly turned her head. When she dared to look again, the old woman was holding the tin cup with both hands, sniffing its contents. She took a cautious sip, then noisily sucked the coffee out. Her satisfaction was evident in the grin she gave the bottom of the cup.

"It's better drunk hot," Rebecca said. "Back home sometimes we put sugar in it, when we had sugar. Back home —"

Back home, there were no Indians any more, and no howling wind that blew day and night, and no sod hut with dirt floor, walls, ceiling, grit always sifting down, mice always getting in. Back home, there were family and neighbors and community and Garvey Morris would never have dared to do what he had done, which was to abandon her, run off and abandon her.

"Have you got a name?" Rebecca patted herself above her heart. "I'm Missis Morris." And God help me. "Missis Rebecca Morris. Ruh-beh-ka. I come out here with my husband last year." And I hate it ....

And as soon as I told him ....

The pain of betrayal almost bent her double on her stool. And he run off, she told her unborn child, and left us here to die by ourselves ....

The old woman held up the cup. Rebecca sat up, brushed away something at the corner of her eye that had threatened to become a tear, smoothed the front of her dress. She moved to the hearth and boiled more coffee. The storm gave no sign of letting up. After awhile, the old woman closed her eyes. Rebecca watched her until convinced that she had fallen asleep, then took down her Bible and read to herself by candlelight.

The storm had abated when the old woman awoke. She experienced a moment's utter bewilderment before it came back to her that she was in the hole in the ground with the white woman. She had never seen a white person before, though she had heard many stories about how strange they were. Her husband had once met some, and her brothers. She stroked one mutilated hand with the other and counted the missing finger knuckles, lopped off in token of mourning. She had been young, smooth-skinned, pretty.

The following morning, Rebecca awoke to find the old woman lying before the hearth, fully stretched out, hands at her sides, as if she had known she would die during the night.

Rebecca spent the day digging a grave on the rise behind the sod hut. It was hard, dirty work. The earth was soft and wet and stuck to the shovel, clung to her feet, dragged at her. It was as though the prairie were trying to suck her under. On three separate occasions, she simply stopped digging, squatted in the mud, and cried like a child. When the job was finished, however, she considered the grave she had scooped out to be a perfectly acceptable one for any Christian and quite an excellent one for any heathen. She placed the old woman in the ground, washed her hands thoroughly, and brought out the Bible.

She read aloud from it over the grave, "Hear my prayer, O Lord," and she raised her voice so that the Lord would be sure to hear her above the moan of the wind, "and let my cry come unto thee. Hide not thy face from me in the day when I am in trouble, incline thine ear unto me, in the day when I call answer me speedily. For my days are consumed like smoke, and my bones are burned as an hearth. My heart is smitten, and withered like grass, so that I forget to eat my bread. By reason of the voice of my groaning my bones cleave to my skin. I am like a pelican of the wilderness. I am like an owl of the desert. I watch, and am as a sparrow alone upon the house top." She closed the book, cleared her throat softly, and said, "Hundred and second Psalm, verses one through seven."

She covered the old woman carefully. She cleaned the shovel when she had finished and took it inside. The wind blew, and blew.

Race Relations

As we approached the downtown bridge, I saw the glow of flames reflected on low clouds to the east. "What's going on?"

The cab driver shrugged and continued to avoid looking at me in the rearview mirror. Bad enough that I was his fare, that I was probably shredding his upholstery; worse if he had to talk to me.

I said, "It looks like the whole east side of town's on fire," and after ten seconds or so the cab driver—suddenly curious, perhaps, about my tipping habits—managed a reply.

"It's rioting. It's on the television."

"I don't have television. Who's rioting?"

Another shrug. "Those people on the east side."

I thought I recognized his accent. "Are you Jamaican?"

His grip tightened on the steering wheel. "American."

"Me, too."

"Like hell," he muttered under his breath. He either didn't know or didn't care that my hearing was enhanced. He had proved his point anyway. "Like hell" was as American as you got.

I let him be and read graffiti on the buildings we passed. You could tell who lived in which neighborhood by what was scrawled on the buildings that bounded it, death to gooks or spics out of u.s. or kill all nigers (sic), liberally seasoned, of course, with swastikas, death's heads, the f-word, and the occasional incongruous heart. My own apartment building on the edge of Kiwi Town, adjoining a poor white neighborhood, was decorated with all the standard threats and insults. For the benefit of casual passersby, we targets of this hostility were helpfully identified by a host of innocuous-seeming terms, gropings toward the one succinct enough, emphatic enough, to put my kind in its place: cockle-burr, eggboy, coconut, hairy turd, beachball, porcupine, pangolin, kiwi. At least my kind had brought out educated bigots. I had to love pangolin.

"Here you go," the cab driver said as we pulled up in front of the Blue Grotto. I handed him money over the seat back, and he took it without turning more than was necessary for him to watch out for my quills. Then I stepped into a humid evening full of sirens and tinged with a faint, not-unpleasant smell of burning. There was little traffic, no one on the sidewalk, few parked cars. The Blue Grotto was dark and cool and elegant, and the hostess was very good, a credit to hostesses everywhere. Had I blinked, I would have missed the flicker of revulsion, the moment of calculation as she wondered how best to shoo away the thing on her doorstep. Nothing so rude as "Go away, you awful monster." More likely, "We require all of our guests to wear a shirt and jacket, and that poncho simply does not qualify"; she could hold out like Horatio at the bridge till I tired of explaining why I can't wear sleeved garments and moved on.

"Miz Barbara Stone," I said quickly, "is expecting me."

"Of course." The situation was under control: I was only a movie actress's exotic date; everyone knew how eccentric movie actresses were. "Please come this way."

There were half a dozen people scattered among the tables. Every one of them gave me a startled look. A man at the back of the room swore just loudly enough for his companion and me to hear. The hostess led me through the room, and I would have kept walking, blundered right into her when she paused and pivoted, if an extraordinarily beautiful Asian woman at a nearby table hadn't called me by name.

It was my turn to be startled. I said, without conviction, "Barbara?"

"Yes. It's me. Really." She looked as Asian as anybody except a real Asian can look. She had always been small, which helped, but now her hair, originally wavy sandy blonde, was straight and as black as a raven's butt. Cosmetic surgery had created delicate folds at the inner corners of her eyes and reduced the dimensions of her nose. Chemicals had changed her complexion. The hostess smiled professionally, shot Barbara a look that meant, *Never bring a pet in here again*, and whisked away. I sat down heavily and tried to locate something of Barbara's old face in her new one. She had always had different faces—her movie-role faces, all of them simulating intimacy and inviting adoration, no two alike save in that they made drunkards give up the bottle, made teetotalers long for a belt, made one pathetic lunatic kill total strangers and himself. She had had her unmade-up, at-home, in-bed, in-love face, too, the one I had liked so much, the one that could make me forget to breathe. She may have been an ambitious, self-absorbed little beauty, but she had been *my* ambitious, self-absorbed little beauty.

The operative phrase here was *had been*.

"My God," I managed to gasp out. "I didn't recognize you."

Barbara made a bright smile and spoke my name again. "No one in the States recognizes me any more. I'm a has-been here. A never-was."

"You—no. You were never a never-was."

"Mm, maybe not. But I am a mega-star all around the Pacific rim now. Oh, it is good to see you."

She sounded sincere, but, then, she was an actress. My heart, which had been hurting ever since I got the call to meet her, started to break. Nevertheless, I put on a smile of my own, probably not a very good one, and said, "You're as lovely as ever. Completely different, but lovely." To spare her having to remark on my own appearance, I added, "When did you decide to become an Asian?"

"Five years ago." Her smile suddenly became a real smile, not the one I remembered, but, still, a real one. Of course. I had directed conversation away from obvious but difficult topics to the subject always dearest to her: her career. "I was rocketing away in the new entertainment capital of the world, when I suddenly bumped my head on a glass ceiling. Things'd reached a point where it was no longer enough for me to be Japanese-speaking and white. I had a choice. I could come back to the States, go down with Hollywood, grub through teevee, dinner theater. Or I could become Japanese-*looking* and be a mega-star overseas."

"You could've looked Japanese with computers."

"That would've been dishonest." Her tone was gently chiding. "I had to become Japanese for real." I would have laughed but for the next thing she said. "I have a Japanese name now, and a Japanese husband."

I couldn't have articulated, even to myself, what I felt at that moment. Whatever it was evidently showed in my face, though, because she looked slightly chagrined and said, "It was a good career move."

"I guess. Well. Are there Japanese kids, too?"

"No. Mister Hara likes my figure the way it is. Anyway, when I heard you'd been found in New Mexico or somewhere, I flew in and called and, well, here I am." She indicated her remade self with an exquisite hand. "This must be very strange for you."

"Everything's strange for me. As for this, I guess it isn't any stranger for a girl from Baton Rouge to play at being Japanese than it ever was for Tokyo businessmen to play at being Texas cowboys. Anyway, the major stuff's easy. Demographic shifts, breakdown of society, people living on the moon, going to Mars. It's the little, personal things that're hard. One minute, I'm twenty-nine years old and have a career and—" I stopped myself from saying *and you.* "The next thing I know, I'm pushing forty-five and don't have anything, and people are telling me I've been possessed for fifteen years by invisible creatures from outer space. Thanks for standing by me, hon."

She looked as though I had slapped her. It took her a moment to make her lower lip stop trembling. "I honestly didn't know. You just left, got up in the middle of the night and left. I didn't know, nobody knew those things were coming and taking over people's bodies. I know you must have a lot of catching up to do. We had something nice, and I was sick with worry about you. But I finally had to get on with my life."

"I got cheated out of my life. Fifteen years of it. Maybe if we'd both been possessed..." Her eyes got as round as they could get. "Forget I said that. It's a horrible thing to wish on somebody."

"Was it, did it—"

"I have no memories of it. None at all."

"Oh."

"I've run into two or three of our old friends. We don't see one another, I just run into them. I'm like some young animal that wandered away from the nest and came back smelling funny. None of my litter-mates really wants to have anything to do with me. But they do sort of try to bring me up to date. I hear about Bill and Sally's two sons, or Bruce and Nancy's daughter, and commit the information to memory like a kid learning the multiplication tables. Eventually, I'll be able to pretend I have something to show for the past fifteen years."

"If there's anything I can do," she said quietly, "to help you catch up, or if you need money—don't be offended. I know the government stipend isn't much. I have more money than I'll ever be able to spend."

I shook my head. "I have enough." Enough for a small room in Kiwi Town and all the spoiled fruit I could eat. I began to strangle on a sob and willed my eyes not to water. Maybe she really had loved me, as crazy as it seemed at the time, but now she was capable only of remembering that she had, whereas I had gone from then to now in a blink. I wanted, and didn't dare, to take her hand. *She'll be repulsed*, I warned myself. *She'll get quills stuck in her.* I godhelpme was still in love with whatever remained of her inside her alien form. It was a relief to notice the hostess moving among the tables. "Barbara," I said, "she's telling everybody the place is closing early. The riot's out of control, spreading. There's no danger here, of course, but a curfew's been announced. You and I had better leave and go lock ourselves indoors."

"We'll finish this conversation another time."

"Yes." I felt a sudden great tenderness for her. It was over between us, she was running a decade and a half ahead of me, had mutated into a stranger I would never get the chance to know, but she had come all this way to see me. She must have, I decided, truly loved me, once upon a time. We rose. "See you around, Barb," I said. "Missis Hara." She spoke my name again, this time as though Mozart had composed it.

Then we went our separate ways, forever.

After several tries, I caught a cab back to Kiwi Town and had myself deposited in front of its one bar. Almost the first thing I had done to mark my alleged return to normal life was to pay a visit to my old neighborhood bar. A neighborhood bar, I reasoned, ideally existed out of time, unchanging, comfortingly static. It turned out to be not such a terrific idea: nobody who hadn't been possessed wanted to drink with anybody who had.

Kiwi Town's bar had no name, no music, and only three bristly customers sitting on stools. There was a television set mounted high in a corner. The sound was turned down; the image on the screen was an aerial view of burning buildings and streets filled with running, falling, crawling human figures. No one paid any attention. Two of my fellow pangolins argued at one end of the bar, and the third sat at the other end staring at nothing I could see and absently stroking his chin quills. The bartender poured me a drink. I let it sit, watched the ice melt, and eavesdropped on the argument, which had to do with whether or not male and female pangolin people would breed true.

"Who do you know," the taller one demanded, "who has sex any more? You even have a sex drive, Jimmy? I sure don't. I don't even miss it until you remind me to think about it. You only think about it because sex is all you ever thought about, back when. So. No sex drive? No breeding. Besides, all the aliens did was enlarge certain glands and organs. Genetically, we're still just human beings."

"Tom, we're not still human *anything!*"

"Listen to me, Jimmy. Acquired traits can't be passed on."

"You're telling me if I got some girl pregnant right now, the baby'd be a normal human baby?" Jimmy slid off his stool and held his arms away from his torso. "Look at me." His voice was plaintive. "*Look* at me, for crissake!"

Tom looked, and so did I, though there was nothing there I didn't see in my mirror every day: a robust, egg-shaped body covered with stiff, spiky hair.

Jimmy noticed me and climbed back onto his stool. "We should've made 'em change us back before they left."

"Nobody could make them do anything," said the man at the opposite end of the bar. He nodded a hello to me. "Haven't seen you in here before."

"I'm—it's only been a couple of weeks since I came to. In the middle of nowhere. Arizona."

"My name's Graham. Call me Al. That's Tom and Jimmy at the far end there, and Dick's the gent behind the bar. We're all the patrons Dick has so far. He doesn't sell much liquor."

"Don't need to," Dick said, favouring me with a smile. "I'm independently wealthy."

"Nice work if you can get it," said Jimmy.

"It eludes me," Al told Dick, "how your heirs and assigns failed to have you declared *non compos mentis* while you were possessed."

Dick shrugged. "What can I say? I got relatives who're idiots. I got a lawyer who eats idiots for breakfast."

Al turned back to me. "And you are—"

"Charles."

"Not Charlie or Chuck?"

"Not any more." Not after Barbara. Not ever again.

"Well, Charles, what do you suppose you were doing in Arizona? You and how many others?"

"Seven or eight hundred. I don't know. Soldiers hustled each of us away as fast as we came to."

Al nodded. "Pretty much the same with me, only I came to in Oslo. Sweden!"

"We were constructing things," I said. "Pushing rocks around, piling them up, moving them around. It didn't make an sense."

"Art," said Al. "I think all of us, all around the world, were creating their art. Maybe not serious art, though. More like the pictures you draw in the sand at the beach."

Jimmy said, "You're nuts."

"Am I?" Al rolled his apparently untasted drink between his palms. "What do you think all the tens, the hundreds of thousands of us on six continents were up to, then?"

Jimmy only swore, but Tom said, "Why didn't they reveal themselves? That's what I want to know."

Al raised a spiny hand. "They did!"

"You know what I mean. Why didn't they try to communicate with us or something? What were they after?"

"Maybe they were after our women and our methane."

Tom scowled. "The most important event in human history, we get visited by Martians or Venusians or whatever, and nobody even knows it's happened until people like us start wandering off and turning into porcupines. There were alien beings moving us around, working us like puppets, and why?" He looked from Al to me to Dick and back to Al. "For what?"

"For their very alien purposes, I imagine," Al said.

"Well, they should've told us things. A race that can travel invisibly between the stars—no flying saucers, just show up—beings like that must have the answers to a lot of big questions. They might not have remembered war."

"How does that follow?" said Al. "We can split atoms. But go outside this neighborhood—" he gestured at the television screen "—and there's utter racial and ethnic Balkanization. Whites hating all non-whites. Blacks, browns, yellows hating all whites. Hating each other, too. The few remaining reds wishing everybody would just go back to Europe, Africa, Asia, and let them have their land back. Under all these stickers I'm a real old fart. I was just a kid back in the days of the civil rights movement, but I was aware enough to pick up on a wonderful idea. The idea was that society would eventually, inevitably become colorblind. That there'd cease to be any hyphenated Americans. We'd all remember where we came from, of course, and take pride in our origins, but we'd all realize who we *were*. Just Americans. Finally, just human beings."

"Oh, brother," Jimmy said.

Tom made an exasperated sound. "I'm not talking about human beings. I'm talking about highly advanced creatures who probably conquered disease—"

"They *were* a disease!"

"—who could've taught us so much."

"Yeah. Like the Europeans taught the Indians."

"Well," Al said, "the aliens obviously didn't come to communicate or establish interstellar trade routes. And they didn't suffer themselves to be studied, quarantined, or killed off, though every government on Earth tried to do each of those things at some point or another." To me, he said, "They deflected violence directed at themselves, you know. I mean, at ourselves. The human race declared war on them, yet they somehow remained at peace with the human race. Lucky for all of us here."

"Lucky, hell!" Jimmy glared the length of the bar. "I had everything before this crap started. Business was great, I had cars, money, women. I had it all. Now I got goddamn quills growing out of me. I give myself the creeps. I live in a goddamn ghetto with two thousand other people who give me the creeps. And all I can eat is goddamn rotten fruit."

"Be grateful," Al said, "they didn't turn you into an insectivore."

"Why don't you stuff a cork in it, old man?"

"Sorry, Jimmy. Even now, I can't speak of aliens and keep an entirely straight face."

I pushed myself away from the bar. Dick cocked an eyebrow and asked gently, "Leaving so soon? You haven't touched your drink."

"Neither has anyone else."

"I don't guess they liked alcohol."

"We come here for the company." Al cast a smile. His gaze settled on the television screen. "I think they were in transit. Going from somewhere to somewhere else. Earth was only a rest stop."

"Well," I said, "they sure messed everything up for me."

"They did that for everybody," Jimmy put in bitterly.

Al said, "I was a geologist. Now I lay tile. You?"

"A voice coach. For movie actors."

"Really?"

"I'm still living off my government stipend and looking for work I can do."

"All the sideshows are full up," said Jimmy. "I know. I checked."

I lurched outside. Several poncho-clad people stood in the street, gazing up at the fringe of sullen red clouds visible above the rooftops. I took two steps, and then Al was suddenly at my side.

He touched my arm lightly and said, "You'll adapt."

"To this? Christ!"

"Look at the bright side. I know, I know—what bright side?" He tapped himself sharply on the chest. "I'm seventy years old, and I feel great. I'm stronger and have more stamina than I did when I was in my twenties. I can hear what people're whispering a hundred yards away. The aliens didn't just modify our bodies, they improved them. Tom was on to one thing back there, the part about conquering disease. We never seem to get sick."

"They stole our lives!"

"True, true. But—listen, I was an oil geologist in Texas when I got possessed. Came to in Sweden, and I don't know how I got there or what I may have done getting there. You ever heard of unconformity? Sediments get deposited layer by layer, so you find your Devonian rocks on top of your Silurian on top of your Ordovician. Sometimes, though, you find your Devonian on top of your Ordovician, due to a combination of erosion and a cessation of sedimentation. Unconformity. That's what my lost years are. The aliens took them from me, but they left other things as payment."

I could listen to him no more. I ran to the end of the block. He didn't pursue, only waved when I looked back, and reentered the bar.

I had come in sight of my apartment building on McCarry Street when a car screeched to a stop nearby. I turned toward it to find myself looking into four very young, very angry faces. Two or three fists were shaken at me, and one of the faces called me a walking turd. A machine pistol appeared in one of the fists. "You want some of this?"

I contemplated the hard round muzzle and waited, letting them scream and threaten. I was astonished by my own calm. I wanted to say or do something to defuse their rage, make some gesture that would convey to these beings of another world that I felt no hatred, meant no harm. I could only stand where I was, however, arms at my sides, unsmiling. It wasn't until the faces had withdrawn and the car was speeding away that I felt afraid.

I went inside and sat at my window. I watched the sky burn for hours, and ate brown bananas.

The Electricity of Heaven

Mr Maury scarcely noticed when Lydia arrived with the food basket. He was too agitated to eat. All morning, he had fluctuated between excitement at the prospect of actually getting out an edition and irritability arising from a flare-up, brought on by the recent rains, of what Mrs Maury called his condition. "Inform Mrs Maury," he brusquely told the girl, "that she is not to expect to see me before this evening."

As the day wore on, however, the possibility of his getting out an edition began to seem distinctly remote. He had been hoarding paper against such time as he might obtain ink. At noon, Dennison, his head printer, had set out hopefully on the trail of a report of a sufficient supply of the next best thing, and though Mr Maury muttered unhappily, he was inwardly more pleased than otherwise. An edition printed with shoe polish on wallpaper was better than no edition at all. But evening came, Dennison did not return, and at last Mr Maury told his loitering employees to go home, he would send the boy around to fetch them when he needed them. The men dispersed to their hotels and lodging houses. Mr Maury withdrew to his long, narrow, untidy office on the second floor. A cold, humid wind was blowing over the town and whistling through cracks around the window frames. He had the boy tend to the stove while he eased himself onto the chair behind his desk. After a time, warmth began to suffuse the room, and the chillgray light slanting through the windows seemed less so.

The windows looked out on Main Street. It was Richmond's one real business thoroughfare, but foot traffic was light this Saturday evening. There was no civilian horse traffic; few horses were civilians any more. Looking up, Mr Maury could see, rising above the facing row of buildings, the columns of the Capitol Building and the spires of the Grace and Broad street churches. He gazed out for almost a minute, drumming his thumbs on the desk blotter, then decided that he could no longer ignore his stomach's angry growling. The basket Lydia had brought was sitting on the floor within leg's reach; he drew it to within arm's reach by hooking its handle with the toe of his boot. In it were a half-moon of cornbread and a small pot of molasses. He groaned. You could get mighty tired of cornbread and molasses when it constituted the bulk of your diet. He broke off a piece of the bread, spooned molasses onto it, chewed mechanically. The boy, Snap by name, watched from a bench in the corner. Mr Maury nudged the basket with his foot and said, around a mouthful, "There's cornbread here. If you're hungry, you help yourself." Snap took a piece of bread from the basket as if he were handling nitroglycerin, retired to the bench, and ate as if he had had nothing to eat all day.

At that, Mr Maury reflected, I guess he hasn't. One thing about being an old man, you don't get so hungry. Comes in handy in times like these. Still—he sighed with true longing—if only I could have a cup of real coffee. And some real printing ink, of course, and newsprint.

When he had finished eating, the boy checked the fire in the stove and then, without so much as a by-your-leave, curled up on the bench and fell asleep. Mr Maury laced his fingers together over his breastbone, settled back in his chair, and let himself go to sleep. It was a fitful rest. His leg did not hurt particularly but would not rest comfortably. From time to time some minor commotion in the street roused him. Upon being roused, he would scoot up in his chair, draw his coat more tightly about himself, gaze around unfocusedly until he remembered to reset his spectacles on his nose.

Once, he awoke to more than usual uproar and, looking out, saw men armed with muskets pass in a ragged column from the direction of Capitol Square. He opened the window and called down to a horseman, "What regiment is that?"

"Regiment?" The horseman made a sound that was as much growl as laugh. "These here's the men from Chimborazo."

Mr Maury frowned. Chimborazo was the military hospital on the heights east of town; the only men from there would be half-sick or crippled soldiers. "Where are you going at this hour?"

"I ask myself that," said the horseman. He peered at the signs adorning the narrow brick front of Mr Maury's building and added, "And even if I knew, I sure wouldn't say in front of a blamed newspaper office." Without another word, he turned his horse and trotted away.

The men from Chimborazo limped by. The procession was quite different from those Mr Maury had watched from this very window four years before. There had been no wounds or sickness then, and the uniforms had been new. Now there were hardly any uniforms at all. Only an idiot would deny that the intervening years had been full of hardships, yet, however transformed by its trials, this was the same army, setting out in defense of the same cause against the same tyranny. It was indomitable spirit, not handsome uniforms, that would bring victory. Profoundly moved, Mr Maury sang out, "God bless you, brave defenders of the Confederacy!" The marching men looked up curiously, their faces indistinguishable blobs in the darkness. One of them called him an old fool and told him to stop his yowling. Another told him to go to bed, Richmonders could sleep secure in the knowledge that the Confederacy still had a few soldiers Grant hadn't entirely killed. Despite their bad humor, Mr Maury watched until all had passed and vanished. He could forgive men who had been through so much.

He returned to his chair, but sleep would not come. At length, with a sigh, he took up a strip of advertising copy from the clutter on his desk and scanned it idly. Under the heading *Negroes for Sale and Hire*, he read,

FOR HIRE—A likely Negro Girl, and a Boy about 15 years old—both good house servants. Apply to THOS J STARKE, 203 Main St.

There were a dozen similar notices in the column. He placed the strip to one side and picked up another, headed *Substitute Notices.*

WANTED—A SUBSTITUTE for a conscript, to serve during the war. Any good man over the age of 35 years, not a resident of Virginia or a foreigner, may hear of a good situation by calling at Mr GEORGE BAGLEY's office, Shockoe Slip, to-day, between the hours of 9 and 11 A.M. A COUNTRYMAN.

WANTED—Immediately, a SUBSTITUTE. A man over 35 years old, or under 18, can get a good price by making immediate application to Room No. 50, Monument Hotel, or by addressing "J.W.," through Richmond P.O.

WANTED—A SUBSTITUTE for the war. A gentleman whose health is impaired, will give a fair price for a substitute. Apply immediately at ROOM, No. 13, Post-Office Department, third story, between the hours of 10 and 3 o'clock.

Mr Maury clicked his tongue in disgust. Now, he thought, addressing himself to A Countryman, J.W., and the gentleman whose health was impaired, Robert Lee is a gentleman whose health is impaired! And where would the Confederate States be if Robert Lee had hired someone to serve in his stead? Mr Maury had inveighed bitterly against the policy of permitting reluctant draftees to hire substitutes. He had written,

It undermines our Army's physical and moral well-being, for not only is the practice subject to abuse, resulting in the replacement of able-bodied fighting men by individuals too old, too young, or too ill meet the Army's needs, and who desert anyway at the first opportunity, but it reinforces the pernicious idea that this is a rich man's war and a poor man's fight. Once cripple a soldier's faith, and he has been decisively

defeated without coming in sight of the Yankees and
their auxiliary hordes of foreigners and negroes...

In the end, however, Mr Maury had had to yield out of
necessity. A man who could pay another man hard money to do his
fighting for him could pay hard money to advertise the fact in the
newspaper. Too many people on the dwindling list of subscribers
were reduced to paying in produce. Not that potatoes and turnips
were to be sniffed at, not when many Richmonders were trying to
subsist on hardtack, but cold cash took some of the effort out of
doing business.

He shoved the offending strip of notices away and reached
for a scrap of butcher paper and a stubby pencil. He had worked
intermittently on his latest broadside since arriving at the office.
It began,

> We are hopeful of the campaign which is opening
> at Petersburg, and trust that we are to reap a large
> advantage from the operations evidently near at hand.

He glanced absently out the window and then started writing.
He wrote steadily but unhurriedly, in a precise and presentable
hand, never looking back, never pausing to make corrections.
After four years of war and almost ten times that number in the
newspaper business, he could write editorials virtually automatically,
drawing on not only an undepleted reservoir of feeling but also an
encyclopedic memory for effective phrases gleaned from numerous
and varied sources. John Daniel of the competing *Examiner* had
once declared that everything Mr Maury read or heard inevitably
made its way out his pen. "Not even the scribblings of Yankees,"
Daniel had gone on, "are beneath his notice or contempt."

John Daniel was a chronically hateful man, and his newspaper
was a seditious rag. Mr Maury had never hesitated to exercise his
right to criticize the government when he perceived the painful
need to do so. But the *Examiner* clearly abused the freedom of
the press, going far beyond criticism to outright vituperation of
everyone charged with the conduct of the war. Ordinarily, Mr
Maury would not have deigned to acknowledge Daniel's existence,
but the attack on *him* had stung. He had *had* to respond publicly:

Even members of the infernal Yankee race—even Old
Abe, the ape himself—occasionally turn a useful phrase,
and it is a patriot's duty to help himself to anything
useful that the enemy might produce. For as one of
those Yankee scribblers has pointed out, this is War!
War to the knife! Knife to the hilt!

To which Daniel had replied, "Maury is a great patriot, but an
even greater parrot."

Well, sir, Mr Maury thought with enormous satisfaction, now
you are the late and unlamented John Daniel, sent at last to your
long account. Report from Hell, unless the devil, too, is tired of
your lies!

He felt sleep trying to reclaim him. He stuffed the pencil and
the butcher paper into a pocket and let it have him. At dawn, he
awoke to the ringing of the tocsin in Capitol Square. It was cold in
the room. Snap had pulled some old newspapers over himself for
warmth. Mr Maury called to him to wake up and see to the fire,
and he dutifully slid out from under his blanket of back numbers
and moved to the stove. The old man was asleep again inside of
two minutes.

He started awake violently at a resounding bang. Mrs Maury
was in his office, brought, it occurred to him in his befuddled
state, by the thunderclap itself. She was flushed and breathless,
and her homemade straw hat was askew. "The most terrible thing!"
She twisted her prayer book in her hands. "Terrible!"

He could only gape at her. Her words were meaningless gabble
in his ears. Her *presence*, however, *here*—

No less disconcertingly, the doorway clogged with skirts and
femininity as the young Dunston twins thrust themselves into
his office. They were his wife's cousins or nieces, he could never
remember which. They, too, were talking excitedly, squealing, in
fact. He heard only the words "horrid" and "awful" and could not
be certain which twin said what; he had never been able to tell
them apart, either. Understanding came to him in bits and pieces
and all out of order. St. James Church was located on the far side
of Capitol Square from the newspaper office, and the women
must have traveled the entire distance on foot and in a hurry,

for a fine film of perspiration gleamed on each face. The sound that awakened him had been hard, sharp, and close by, nothing like the muffled thump of a siege gun—only the sound of a door's being flung back on its hinges. And the sun was up, well up, it was midday, he had slept away the morning at his desk. He licked his dry lips and ran a hand through his thin white hair. The Dunstons' squeals subsided as their attention was drawn irresistibly to their exotic surroundings; it took a moment for the general untidiness and inkiness of the office to register on them, and then, to the accompaniment of dismayed little sounds, *ooh*, they drew their arms up and in, close to their sides, and crossed their wrists over their girlish bosoms to protect their precious gloves. Lydia appeared behind them and peered in as well. Her expression, at least, was composed under its moist sheen.

Why don't I sell tickets, he thought, greatly irritated, and give a lecture tour? Beyond being irritated, he was deeply shocked. He would never have said it aloud at home, but his office was the only place where he was assured of peace and quiet any more, and not simply because his press was idle more often than not. Dutifully, uncomplainingly, had he given over his home to a legion of mostly female relatives, whom the enemy's depredations had left no choice but to come as refugees to Richmond. Until now, his wife had not, in all their years of marriage, entered the shop. No woman—Lydia did not count—had so much as stuck her head into his office on the second floor.

"Samuel," his wife gasped, "we are lost!"

"Lost!" echoed one or both of the Dunston girls.

Mr Maury reached out and took his wife's hand. "Please calm down, Clara, and catch your breath. Then tell me—"

Mrs Maury pulled her hand away sharply and started talking in a rush, punctuating her speech with impatient gestures. "After services, as we came out of church, we met Doctor Channing, who had run over from the Episcopal Church. He said that during the communion address, the sexton gave a message to President Davis, who left as soon as he read it. Then—"

"The president's duties have often called him away from services."

"—General Anderson was called away next, and the pastor himself left the chancel." She appeared not to have heard a word he said. "Well, as Doctor Channing said, by this time, what was anybody to think? Something frightful must have occurred."

"Whatever it is, I'm sure the president will soon have the matter in hand."

"Someone said the army is retreating from Petersburg!"

That touched off a fresh duet of squealing by the Dunstons. Mr Maury held up his hands, palms out, to ward off the noise and said, flatly, "Impossible."

"If Lee's army is retreating," Mrs Maury said, "the Yankees are going to march right into Richmond, looting and burning, and every negro in town will—"

She cut herself short and turned toward Lydia, whose expression remained composed. After a moment, the girl dropped her eyes under the weight of her mistress' stare. In the corner, the boy looked on placidly. Mr Maury could read nothing in their expressions. Yet, he thought, something must be passing through those woolly heads. Everything has changed so fast, everything is different now. He could still feel, after two weeks, the tingle of unease he had experienced upon seeing companies of negro troops, the Confederacy's first, drilling on Capitol Square. They had had no uniforms and had not looked as though they would ever amount to anything. Even so... Bad enough that Richmond was no longer the quiet, lovely town he had known and loved all his life, that one could not enter the streets without encountering all the rabble and trash who had arrived since the commencement of hostilities. But negro troops! And in the square, the heart of the sacred Confederacy! Mr Maury had had all he could do on that occasion to resist the impulse to cry out, "No, sir!"

He glanced down at his cluttered desktop, and his eye settled gratefully on a copy of the *Petersburg Daily Express*. He snatched it up and gave it a shake.

"A courier gave me this last night," he said. "He'd just come from Petersburg. It's yesterday's edition, and look here!" He laid his finger on a particular block of copy. "A summation of the situation at Petersburg by observers *in* Petersburg. Who could be better placed to say what is going on down there? 'Our lines are secure against all attacks of the enemy,' it states here. And here— 'On the whole all goes well with us and 'ere long we hope to be able to chronicle a glorious victory for our arms and a crushing defeat to the enemy.' It can only mean that Johnston's bringing his army up from North Carolina to join Lee. So, you see, you mustn't pay attention to sensational rumors. They'll only confuse you and make you prey to panic."

His wife regarded him dubiously, the Dunstons, frightenedly.

"McClellan," Mr Maury said, "was almost at our gates in 'sixty-two, and Lee sent him packing. And I've visited the Petersburg line. Lee's fortifications would discourage Napoleon himself."

"That General Grant," said Mrs Maury, "seems harder to discourage than McClellan and Napoleon both!"

"Very well. I'll go to Capitol Square myself and find out exactly what the situation is."

The doubt in his wife's expression intensified. "Samuel, you'd do better to come home right now. A man your age, with your condition—I'm certain you've done yourself quite enough harm sleeping in a hard chair in this drafty place without—"

"It's not so bad now." He turned, picked up his hat and cane, and beckoned to Snap. "If there's a real emergency, *if*, I'll send the boy to you. In the meantime, please don't do anything foolish."

Mrs Maury gave him her severest look, with eyebrows lowered and mouth set in a tight-lipped, mirthless smile. Forty-three years of marriage had impressed the look's meaning upon him: her mind was now made up, he could do nothing to change it. "I am *not* going to wait for instructions," she said. "I apprehend violence from those Yankees, and I intend to make my preparations now!"

She turned from him like a top and hustled the Dunstons away. Lydia stepped aside so that her mistress and the young ladies might pass, then fell in behind them.

Mr Maury looked down at the boy and said, "Come with me, Snap, and try to keep up."

His mood improved as soon as he stepped outside. The day was bright, beautiful, and fragrant with the smells of spring. He found that he could not even be irritated with Snap, who barely concealed his impatience with his master's slow pace. In fact, it seemed to Mr Maury that he was the only person in the street who was not in a hurry. He depended heavily upon his stout silver-headed cane as he labored up the sloping street. He had lied to his wife; in truth, his condition was bad enough today. The pain had its own system. It shot up his thigh right into the hip socket, paused to reload, then shot again. Any more, he would not have been too proud to hitch a mule to the family trap, if he had had a mule, but not even mules had escaped impressment. It was walk or stay put.

Still, he was not one to complain. Lee was said to suffer from rheumatism, and to suffer it with manful stoicism, and Mr Maury was pleased to emulate the example of the South's most glorious hero. All the same, the general still had his Traveller and could ride wherever he wanted to go. The entire Maury household had been afoot all winter. Well, sacrifices had to be made.

At the end of the block, all of a hundred yards from his printing establishment, he looked toward the Capitol and saw a tendril of smoke rising and curling above the intervening rooftops. He started walking again, faster than before, though not really very fast at all. Governor Street was full of civilians dressed for Sunday services and, here and there, a gray- or butternut-jacketed soldier. A bonfire blazed in the middle of the pavement, and the crowd milled around it anxiously, like animals about to stampede. Mr Maury turned toward 9th Street and was astonished to see that the banks were open. He grabbed at the sleeve of a man whom he knew to be associated with the Traders' Bank and demanded, "What has happened?"

The man tried to brush off Mr Maury's hand and kept looking past his face, toward the river and the bridges leading to Manchester. "General Lee's been killed," he said, "and the army's running away! Abandoning us! The Yankees'll be in Richmond tomorrow!"

Mr Maury looked after him sourly, then down at the boy. "Don't you mind what that man says."

Within himself, he felt a chill of dread. He remembered the shock of Stonewall Jackson's death. He had not believed that news at first, either. No one had, but Mr Maury had gone so far as to dismiss the first report in his newspaper as a scaremongering tactic intended by Yankee sympathizers to tarnish the great victory at Chancellorsville and demoralize loyal citizens.

He halted again when he reached the 9th Street side of the square. There were bonfires and too many people there, too. A line of excited spectators stretched for a block in either direction from St. Paul's Church at the corner of Grace. Men were staggering out of the government buildings across from the church with armloads and boxloads of papers. These they dumped onto the fires. Sparks flew up and turned in the air. The line of spectators writhed.

Mr Maury recognized one of the clerks from the War Department. "Hoehling! Burke Hoehling!"

The man turned. He was red-faced and sweaty from exertion, and the whiskers, eyebrow, and hair on the right side of his head were badly singed.

"There are rumors," said Mr Maury, "wild rumors that Lee's been killed, the army's been routed."

Hoehling upended a wooden box full of papers over the fire and stood back to admire the effect. "Well, something's sure happened. Richmond's being evacuated. The government's moving to Danville this evening."

Mr Maury licked his lips. It was like licking tree bark; there was no moisture on his tongue or in his mouth. "I'm sure," he said, "I'm sure Lee is all right. I'm sure he has the situation in hand."

"If I was you—well, it's a safe bet the Federals'll hang any patriotic white man they catch. As a' early secessionist, you're bound to be on their list. My advice is, get out of the city. Hire a horse or wagon if you can."

"Won't there be room on the trains? I have a house full of women and children."

"There won't hardly be room for the government, let alone families. Probably won't even be room for me. There's just the one line open to Danville, and six run-down locomotives, and it's up to the bureau chiefs which clerks get evacuated." Hoehling showed his teeth in what could have been a grin or a grimace.

"We boxed these archives weeks ago in anticipation of just this development. Now we got to unbox 'em and burn 'em, because we can't take 'em with us. How's that for organization? Everything boxed and ready to go, but no place for it to go to, and no way to get it there. When I finish here, I'm just going to walk off to the west. You might try to get your family out on the Kanawha canal."

Mr Maury nodded slowly. "If not... I am obliged to remain here."

"Well, you may just be putting your own head through a Yankee noose."

"I must protect my family to the best of my ability. There are negro troops in Grant's army."

Hoehling scowled. "Well, whatever you do, you'd better get down to Bank Street and get your specie out. You ain't likely to find anyone who's going to take paper in any quantity, 'less it's Federal greenbacks."

Mr Maury drew himself up slightly. "I've never approved of using notes issued by the very people who are trying to enslave us."

"Don't get so stiff." The clerk gestured in no particular direction. "Over there, they're burning bales of unsigned treasury paper." He wiped his hands on his waistcoat and offered one. "Good luck to you, sir."

Mr Maury hesitated for a second before shaking the hand. "And to you."

The clerk turned to his bonfire. Mr Maury took the boy by the shoulder and moved on. Further along he caught sight of a well-dressed little man so bent and twisted in body that he was virtually a hunchback. This bowed individual's hair stuck out untidily from beneath his hat, framing a yellowish, withered face that had always put Mr Maury in mind of a monkey's. When Mr Maury called to him, addressing him as Mr Vice President, the face twitched and put on an expression of extreme annoyance.

"Maury, is it?" Alexander Stephens' voice was sharp, almost shrill.

"There's a rumor that Lee has been killed."

"He was alive enough to send the president a telegram this morning."

"Then it *is* just a rumor! Thank God! And is the army still behind its fortifications?" When the other man hesitated, Mr Maury burst out angrily, "The news, sir, if you please!"

"I should think you would be in your office now," Stephens drawled, "*inventing* news, as usual."

"I know we have had our differences in the past," Mr Maury said hotly, "but we are, both of us, patriotic Southerners. I ask you as a countryman to tell me what is going on."

"Why, chaos." Stephens swept the scene before them with a bony yellow hand like a chicken's claw. "If you want a more optimistic report, I suggest you ask the president. You'll find him roaming about. He's been roaming about ever since he heard from Lee this morning. I just now saw him on Broad Street, by the African Church, of all places. He told the congregation that today's disasters are temporary, and we will soon come back to establish the capital in Richmond. He told them that victory for the South is inevitable, but they must have courage and faith."

"I am glad to hear that President Davis, at least, hasn't given up hope."

Something like a smile flickered at the corner of Stephens' mouth, "President Davis is your match for pertinacity, but I daresay he could have picked a more likely audience for his little speech. The African Church!"

"I'm sure he was just trying to keep them from becoming excited."

"I would have expected them to be dancing for joy, but there never was such a crowd of strangely somber blacks. The whole congregation was in the yard, but standing back from the street. They had the look of people guarding a secret. Quiet, watchful."

"Watching for Old Abe himself to come riding by, I expect!"

The vice president frowned thoughtfully. "He may well do it now. Lee's army has been driven from its positions."

"Nonsense! That army's never been routed. If Lee's pulled back at all, he's pulled back in good order."

A spot of color appeared on Stephens' cheek. "Lee hasn't pulled back, he's been pushed out!"

Mr Maury was choking, his eyes were tearing uncontrollably. He coughed and waved a hand before his face. Surely it was only a wisp of smoke. A smudgy pall was collecting among the branches of the trees in the square. Roiling smoke obscured the equestrian statue of George Washington. "Probably," he croaked, "probably Lee is just shortening his line. He's going to draw Grant out into the open, where he can whip him, just like he whipped McClellan, Hooker, and the rest. We have to believe in Lee!"

"Lee's beaten! *We're* beaten!"

"God will protect the right! God will send the electricity of Heaven to fall with destructive violence upon the serried host of the enemy!"

The vice president shook his head, made to turn away, then leaned forward and said, "What you believe is of no moment to me. Good day, sir. Goodbye!"

Poisonous little gnome! thought Mr Maury as Stephens walked away. Damned hunchback!

He led Snap back down Capitol Hill. Progress slowed to a creep when they entered Main Street. As Mr Maury ploughed across the thoroughfare, parting the mass with his shoulder, like an ice-breaker, while trying to hold on to hat, cane, and boy with one too few hands, he felt certain that every hotel and saloon in Richmond must have turned itself inside out. The entire spectrum of the criminal fraternity was on parade, flashily dressed idlers and hangers-on, gamblers, rowdies, extortionists, deserters, skulkers, croakers, pickpockets, prostitutes, profiteers, drunkards, free negroes, foreigners, shoving decent citizens against the walls, stalling traffic, creating a pandemonium. His weaving path intersected that of a trader herding several dozen slaves. The slaves were chained by the ankles and made a jingling racket as they shuffled along. The trader, clearly approaching a state of panic, was prodding them with his stick. He wiped his face on his coat sleeve and poked savagely at the nearest slave, and to Mr aury he said, "Never *seen* such a dawdling pack of niggers!"

Mr Maury, who had always felt himself to be a good master, said, "God will hold a man to account for treating slaves with justice."

"Infernal busy-body!" the trader shouted, spraying tobacco spittle. "Get out of my way!"

Mr Maury reached the door of his building and plunged gratefully into its gloomy, pungent interior. He locked the door, went upstairs to his office, and opened the safe. Inside were an assortment of loose papers and a tin box. He opened the box and pawed through its contents—paper money and a handful of coins. He had had no hard money deposited in any bank since the third year of the war. There were only these few coins and a few more like them at home. Such specie as substitute notices and advertisements for servants brought into his establishment almost always and almost immediately passed out of it again, as wages for his skeletal force of reporters, compositors, and printers, and in payment of ever costlier printing supplies, firewood, and groceries.

He pocketed the coins, returned the notes to the box, and tucked it under his arm. He and the boy re-entered the street as a ripple of excitement spread through the crowd. "What is it?" he demanded of no one in particular. "What is it now?"

A few people babbled incoherently at him as they passed. A swarthy man drew up and said, "They say the Federals has broken Lee's line at Five Forks!"

"Who says?"

"I overheard a dispatch rider say it down by the Spotswood. He'd just come from Ewell's headquarters! The Federals enveloped Pickett at Five Forks and cut him off from Lee!"

"Pickett! Might have known. He's failed Lee before. The man's as useless as a free nigger! Come, Snap, keep up!"

They hurried on. Cary Street, below Main, was even more crowded. Just as they reached it, there came a fresh surge of excitement—the government commissary was being opened for all who wanted food. People froze in mid-motion for a moment, amazed, and then the old man and the boy found themselves caught in the push and tug of a dense human course. Most of the city's factories and warehouses were located along Cary. As though by conjuration, a brigade of the city's poor appeared. It struck Mr Maury that every impoverished household in Richmond, black as well as white, must have been waiting to disgorge its contingent of hollow-eyed men, starveling women, and ragged children. They moved quickly, purposefully, and noisily, with bags, baskets, buckets, tubs, tin pans, and aprons at the ready, and converged on the doors of the various depots.

Those fortunate enough to have been first into the depots soon began to emerge from them. Some found themselves running vicious gantlets of individuals unfortunate enough to have been at the rear of the mob. A woman rushed by Mr Maury hugging a sack of flour as though it were a beloved child; her dress had been torn literally to ribbons, and there was a sort of exalted terror in her expression. Another woman leaped into her path. The second woman was carrying a black iron frying pan, which she swung edge-on. The first woman uttered a bleat of pain that was barely audible against the general howl and dropped her prize. Her attacker snatched it up and hugged it no less tenderly as she ran away.

Others managed to escape unscathed and with their booty intact. Some of the gauntest women and children Mr Maury had ever seen staggered by bearing astonishing armloads of flour, bacon, sugar, and coffee, and after them came others, singly and in teams, tumbling boxes and rolling barrels too heavy to carry away.

Another jostling, desperate mob had formed at the packet landing on the Kanawha canal. The surface of the canal itself was thick with barges, skiffs, and boats. Some craft, already underway, were so heavily loaded with passengers that they were barely afloat. Mr Maury gradually worked his way to the front and unexpectedly found himself facing a burly bargeman who stood at the top of a gangplank and rhythmically tapped the barrel of a revolver against his palm. Standing on deck nearby were two other bargemen and, crowded amidship, a jumble of gentlemen, ladies, children, servants, and luggage of every description.

A whiskery man next to Mr Maury was arguing with the bargeman. He had set his foot on the gangplank. Behind him was a frightened-looking woman who held a crying girl by the hand. He drew them forward, so that the bargeman could see them, and said, "For the love of God—"

"The love o' God's got nothin' to do with it!" The beat of the gun barrel tapping against the bargeman's open hand remained steady. "This boat's for Albemarle, and no one gets on but pays my price. I'll shoot anybody that thinks otherwise. Now take your foot off the plank."

The whiskery man's face mottled above his beard, and he appeared ready to say more, then to think better of it. Clamping his mouth shut, he removed his foot from the gangplank, turned, and pushed a way through the crowd. The woman took the child in her arms and followed.

"Who's next?" the bargeman roared.

"I need transport for myself," Mr Maury said, "and for the members of my household." He reached into his box and pulled out the entire wad of bills.

The bargeman laughed scornfully when he saw what they were. "I can blow my nose on treasury paper!"

"The devil fetch you!"

The bargeman answered with a gap-toothed snarl. "Next!"

Another citizen pushed forward to the gangplank, almost shoving Mr Maury into the canal in the process. He produced a wallet and pulled out a number of U.S. greenbacks. "Passage for myself!"

The bargeman beckoned the citizen forward, and he moved up the gangplank. At the top, he was relieved of the greenbacks and welcomed aboard with much exaggerated and mocking obsequiousness on the part of the two bargemen on deck.

"Who's next?"

Mr Maury pointed his cane at the bargeman. "You are nothing but a damned jew!" He called out to the people huddled together on the boat, "I advise you not to risk your lives with these men! Look! See how low the boat already sets in the water! It won't get two miles before it sinks!"

The motion of the gun barrel stopped. The bargeman regarded him intently. "You're gettin' to be a blister, old man. I won't waste a bullet on you. I'll just break you up and use you for tinder."

The other bargemen laughed.

Mr Maury worked his way crabwise across the landing. Snap stayed close on his heels. At length, they came upon a bench, and Mr Maury collapsed onto it with a groan of relief. The boy seated himself on the ground. As he waited for his legs to stop trembling, the old man surveyed the scene on the landing with mounting disgust and anger. Finally, the question that had been forming in his mind would no longer be denied. His gaze fixed on a point somewhere above and beyond the multitude of heads, on a point between the nearby arsenal and the relatively more distant Tredegar Iron Works, and he asked himself, Even if I were to secure passage for everyone in the household, how could I possibly herd Mrs Maury and all of those young women and babies across town, on foot, through such a howling rabble?

He muttered the answer, and when he saw the boy look up expectantly, he repeated it as if explaining something to an equal: "I can't, it's impossible."

He felt oddly relieved. He took a deep breath and stood up. He told Snap, "Let's go home."

The rioting on Cary Street raged unabated. The rioters seemed not to have got into the liquor warehouses yet, but Mr Maury knew that it was only a matter of time. He and the boy paused in the slight shelter afforded by a doorway, and as the old man struggled to catch his breath, he saw something that alarmed him as much as the thought of the liquor stores did. It was late afternoon, the light was fading, shadows were lengthening and deepening along the street. The Richmond gas works had been shut down. People were now beginning to pillage by the light of whatever torches they could improvise on the spot.

A young army officer wearing a bedraggled plumed hat loomed before him. He had a ham under his arm, and his face was contorted with fury. "Th' army's hungry an' half-naked as a tramp," he bellowed into Mr Maury's face, "an' every damn thing it needs 's been sittin' *here!* God *damn* civilians!" He gave Mr Maury a rough shove as he passed, and the old man would have fallen if someone behind him had not caught him under the arms.

"Go get yourself trampled somewheres else!" his rescuer yelled into his ear.

"That young cavalry rascal almost rode me down!"

"Strode you down's more like it, Grandpa!"

"Let me help you with that, Grandpa!" said another voice.

The tin box was torn from his grasp. It burst open on the pavement, and a vicious little free-for-all erupted. Mr Maury got in the way of a fist; the blow, a glancing one across his cheekbone, sent his spectacles flying and spun him against a wall. He huddled there with his knees clutched to his chest. The struggling, blurrily defined figures before him separated; there was a moment's pause, abruptly punctuated by a howl of disappointment. Someone leaned in close to Mr Maury, flung a handful of paper money into his face, and seized his lapel.

"What's in your pockets?"

"All the money I have is in that box!"

"Let's just see, Methuselah!"

Hands were at his pockets. He swatted them away, felt tension on his watch fob, felt it released as the chain broke. He opened his mouth to protest, but he was knocked hard against the wall again, and his complaint came out in a wheeze. He tried to crawl away, His hand came in contact with the tin box, lying in a litter of paper. He scooped up a wad of money and thrust it into a pocket. He was scrambling for a second handful when he realized that he had lost the boy.

"Snap! Snap!"

Nearby, a thin black stick emerged through a gap in the pushing, cursing mass of bodies. Five delicate twigs on the end of the stick wiggled. Mr Maury reached up, closed his hand on the stick, and pulled. Snap tumbled through the gap, into his arms. He was astonished at how little the boy weighed, how small he really was. They fell back against the wall, and after they had lain there panting for a time, Snap pressed something into his hand—his spectacles. They had been stepped on, the wire frame bent, one lens knocked out. "Bless you, Snap," he said as he perched them precariously on his nose. "You're a good boy."

He squinted through the surviving lens, blinked, got slowly to his feet. With an urgent word to the boy, he began edging along the wall, feeling his way, keeping his good eye on the street. When they had reached the end of the wall, he waited, gathering his strength, then went across Cary at what was, for him, a bone-jarring gallop.

They reached his house well after dark. From the street, it looked abandoned. Fear gnawed at Mr Maury as he approached, and then a sense of relief washed through him when he found the front door locked. He fumbled out his key, entered, and heard a murmur of talk and motion inside. He could not quite make out words, but the sound was comforting. He leaned against the door and heaved a great sigh. Nothing could touch him now. To the boy, who had fallen sullen with weariness, he said, "Go get yourself some supper."

The sound of his wife's voice led him to the parlor. She was standing almost at the center of the room, holding a carved music box, turning in place to survey the furnishings, and issuing a steady stream of detailed instructions for collecting and hiding valuable things. Hurrying about her was at least a company of young women and children. Everyone stopped suddenly and stared at him. He went to Mrs Maury and drew her against himself. She felt stiff and resisting at first but relaxed after a moment and pressed her cheek against his breast. "Lydia," he heard her say, "fetch Mr Maury's spare spectacles."

"I'm fine. Fine."

Mrs Maury pulled away. When he let her go, she stepped back into a semicircle of silent women and girls. The younger children were already losing interest in him and starting to fidget.

"Escape from the city," he announced, "is impossible."

"We know," said his wife. "We knew. Where would we have escaped *to?*"

"But there's nothing to be afraid of, ladies. If the Yankees get into town as far as Church Hill—notice I say *if*, because Lee's sure to spring an unpleasant surprise on them. But if they do come before he lights into them, I'll just cane any Yankee who so much as sets foot in our street."

That elicited a brave smile here and there, but his wife turned away impatiently, clapped her hands to get everyone's attention, and began issuing her instructions again. The better part of a minute passed before Mr Maury perceived that he was in the way. He went away thinking to find himself some supper and hoping against hope that he would not have to settle for cornbread and molasses.

The night passed dreadfully. Everyone was exhausted, yet none of the adult members of the household could think of sleep, and even the children went to bed under protest. The women moved about like rustling ghosts, avoided the downstairs windows, spoke in whispers. Precious candles burned down. The rooms grew cold.

Alone in an upstairs room that looked out over the city, Mr Maury watched fires spread along the waterfront, helped by a strong breeze from the south. He could not be sure, for he missed his timepiece and Mrs Maury had hidden all of the clocks, but he thought that it was about midnight when he heard a whistling of railroad engines. The evacuation trains were rolling. By then, flames spouted from every window of the great flour mills along Cary Street, and the conflagration in the lower part of the city appeared to be general.

Some time later, there was a great flash of light at the window, followed an instant later by the loudest sound he had ever heard. It was like the persistent, reverberating rumble of an earthquake. Window glass rattled. The house itself swayed and trembled.

The sound abruptly died away to something that was not quite silence. No less abruptly, his wife burst into the room, with an indeterminate number of distraught young women in her wake. She might have been reenacting, in pantomime, her arrival at his newspaper office; her mouth worked, yet he heard nothing. He was on his feet, though he had no memory of rising from his chair. He turned toward the window and saw, in the direction of the arsenal and the iron works, a pillar of flame and smoke rising above the blazing waterfront. The flashes of countless lesser explosions filled that quarter of the sky like fireworks, illuminating a low overcast.

Then his ears popped, and he could quite clearly hear the noise of secondary explosions and the uproar in his own house. "What *is* it?" his wife was saying. "Are the Yankees so close that they can bombard the city?"

"I don't know!" he said. "Perhaps they have obliged us by blowing themselves up!"

Mrs Maury and the other women edged past his chair to the window and peeked out. Mr Maury heard one of them say, "It's like the Biblical prophecy of the end of the earth," and another of them answer, "It *is* the end of the South."

"Get away from that window!"

They turned, wide-eyed, startled by his hoarse vehemence.

"Go to your rooms! All of you!"

They moved toward the door, all save Mrs Maury. She stepped between them and her husband.

"Samuel," she said, "don't you think—"

"Stay away from the windows!"

Mrs Maury compressed her lips. She turned her back and walked straight out of the room. The young women mutely followed. Mr Maury remained by the window until the house had quietened and the cataclysm at the arsenal begun to subside, then went back to his chair. After a time, he remembered something, pulled a wad of dirty paper from his pocket, and delicately picked it apart. It consisted mostly of treasury notes, in denominations ranging from one dollar to five hundred dollars, payable to the bearer from six months to two years after the ratification of a treaty of peace between the Confederate States and the United States. Mixed in with these were notes drawn on the state treasuries of Virginia and North Carolina and some fifty-cent shinplasters he had collected as change in transactions with local businesses.

At the bottom of his pocket he found a piece of butcher paper and a pencil. He turned these in his hands as if seeing them for the first time. By the candle's amber glow he read:

> We are hopeful of the campaign which is opening at Petersburg, and trust that we are to reap a large advantage from the operations evidently near at hand.

He took the pencil, scratched out the words *evidently near*, and read on.

> Yet it is painful to observe that a certain degree of despondency is stealing over our people, especially here in Richmond. What is there in the present aspect of affairs, other than there has been from the opening of the war, to make us despond? What are we suffering now which we ought not to have anticipated and which indeed did not we anticipate? Did we not know from the first, at least, did not everybody foresee, except for a few gentlemen claiming to be wiser than all the rest of the world, that the war would be long, desperate,

and tedious? We have had losses, and they are neither small nor few in number. We are somewhat straitened for provisions. Who, among us all, ever expected that it would be otherwise in the course of the war? When we entered upon it, we took all its chances. We embraced them all without hesitation, as the only alternative left, unless we chose to submit to the Yankees without a struggle. Should they all descend upon us in their turn, or at once, we were prepared to stand the brunt of their combined assault, for we know that, by holding out to the end we must triumph, and that not to triumph would mean to be ruined root and branch, body and soul. Well, we have held out for four years against the most tremendous power ever exerted by any one nation since the world was made. One has only to read the records of battles and campaigns in which the Bible abounds to see how frequently, how generally indeed the weaker party in numbers and materiel of war came out victorious.

He let the pencil hover over the paper while he searched through his mental file for a ringing finale. His eyes closed. When he opened them again, the window framed a rectangle of smudgy gray sky. The pencil had slipped from his fingers, fallen to the floor, and come to rest against the baseboard. From the window, he saw that the roofs of the big flour mills had fallen in. He could not be sure, but the fire seemed to have climbed Capitol Hill as far as the square itself. He wondered if he still had a newspaper office. He wondered if Dennison had ever located that store of shoe polish.

He looked down into the street as half a dozen threadbare Confederate cavalrymen come trotting by on horses too weary to go faster. The riders did not have the appearance of soldiers who knew precisely where they were going or what they were about. They seemed almost to skulk. The officer riding at their head rested the barrel of his Colt's Navy across his saddle and kept looking nervously back over his shoulder.

Mr Maury hastened downstairs. Lydia and Snap appeared in a doorway leading to their room at the back of the house. Their faces were drawn with exhaustion. They stood close together in the doorway, she with her hand draped over the boy's shoulder in a gesture as protective as a mother's.

He rushed by them, hesitated at the front door for a moment, then stepped outside. The cold air tasted ashy. There were a few people in the street, a few more visible at upper-floor windows. The cavalrymen had ridden out of sight, but foot soldiers were approaching from the direction the riders had come. No, sir! Mr Maury thought when he saw who they were. No, *sir!*

They were blue-jacketed colored troops, moving at the quick step toward Capitol Square. Mr Maury stepped forward to block their path. Let the army and the government run away! If I only am left to defend the heart of the sacred Confederacy, so be it!

But that heart was a rubble-strewn field of cinders now, and the expressions on the faces of these soldiers showed unmistakeably that they knew they had done a big thing. The men at the front of the column grinned at him. He stepped backward to let them pass. They would not have paused for a thousand symbolic defenders, or a million.

AUTHOR'S NOTE: Although this story's pertinacious protagonist is little concerned with the niceties of attribution—and, moreover, both he and his unnamed newspaper are fictitious—the author is obliged to mention that the advertisements and most of the editorial matter quoted herein are taken almost verbatim from actual Richmond newspapers of the day.

Dog in the Manger

My three mad visitors have their orders, and I am powerless to stop them. They have worked hard in their armor all afternoon, moving through the Unipolitan Center, randomly tearing paintings from walls and raking books from shelves, setting their bombs and thermite charges. All that is needed now is the pressure of a finger on a button in the cabin of their waiting helicraft. They have their orders.

They make me don some sort of protective clothing under the staring blank eyes of Michelangelo's David. David's expression is one of infinite sadness, it seems to me, commingled with contempt for these men and what they are about. I silently bid him a heartbroken farewell. Two of the soldiers fall into position on either side of me, and the third, the lieutenant, precedes us through the art gallery.

As we walk, music by Vivaldi throbs from the walls. The lieutenant amuses himself by shooting off statues' bronze breasts and marble genitalia; he never misses. I cry out in agony as an age-worn gargoyle that once graced a European cathedral is vaporized. I stumble and almost collapse as the last extant Rodin crumbles at the touch of fire from the lieutenant's wand, and one of my escorts has to grip my arm to keep me on my feet. I can only watch as stone nymphs disintegrate into piles of dust, as gold-leaf turns to molten butter.

Just within the massive portals of the Center, we pause while the lieutenant tensely signals his flying machine. "Any sign of them?" he says into a disk on his wristband, and when the answer comes, a crisp *No. sir*, he makes a relieved sound. We leave the building and crunch across the gray, brittle ground toward the helicraft.

Looking back over my shoulder at the great museum that has been my home and my work for so many years, I'm again appalled to see how pitted and scarred its face has become. The invaders have not been kind to it, though what they have done is nothing compared with what these men with me are about to do. I seek solace where I can: the building *is* in considerably better shape than any around it; it still stands. A hold for our greatest treasures, our grandest achievements, a keep impregnable even against the invaders' fire-storms, the Unipolitan Center was made to last a millennium, a dozen millennia. But what people have made other people can unmake.

I lived and worked within the walls of the Unipolitan Center for thirty-one years. I had comfortable quarters there. I led a quiet, satisfying life there. The great masterpieces of art, music, and literature were mine to cherish and protect. Within the walls of the museum, it was easy to ignore the sprawling megalopolis without. It was easier still to ignore vague rumors about some kind of trouble ten, fifteen, however many light-years away.

When *they* came from deep space, however, hounding the tatters of Earth's starfleet like a cloud of maddened hornets, and pushed through the rings of defense satellites, my staff fled in panic, deserted me, deserted the museum, and were consumed in the holocaust. I sealed my home against the searing of the world and listened to programs of Bach and Mozart.

Then they passed, moved on across the face of Earth, razing it as they went. The fire-storms outside the Unipolitan Center burnt themselves out. I emerged alone but unscathed, and the blackened but unbreached fortress of the Center towered proud and defiant above the charred ruins of the greatest city in human history.

When the soldiers came; I ran out to embrace them in their grimy metal-foil suits. Later, after their lieutenant had read me his orders, I called every low thing I could put tongue to, ignorant, unenlightened, barbaric, idiots, savages, monsters. It did no good.

There is a fourth soldier waiting in the helicraft. He helps me clamber aboard, the others follow, and with a whir of quickening rotor blades the machine rises into the sky.

"Oh God, why?" I sob, pressing my face against a small window for a last glimpse of my museum. "In the name of Heaven, why must you do this terrible thing?"

The lieutenant looks at me seriously. "You've got to understand," he says, and his voice is bleak with the strain of the past few days, "it's all over for us. You and me and these other guys, some more people back at headquarters, we're just about the only ones left now. We'll last another week, I guess, another month if we're real lucky, but it's *finished* for us. They've beaten us into the ground, man. Never should've tangled with them. We never had a goddamn *chance*. So what they'll do, they'll come around the planet one more time, give the place a last good working over to make sure they get us all, and then they'll land and start poking around in the ashes. They'll want to know who we were to go barging into their territory in the first place. They'll want to get some idea of what kind of creatures they've just killed off. But we—"

"Lieutenant," says the soldier who is piloting the helicraft, "we got enough altitude on it now. You wanna be the one brings it down?"

"Just push the goddamn button, will you?" is the lieutenant's weary reply, and I watch, paralyzed and speechless with horror, as the pilot shrugs, turns back to his console, depresses a button with his thumb. I close my eyes. From afar comes a muted peal of rolling thunder.

I think of Griffith and Bergman, Kurosawa and Kubrick, Duvall and Burden, hissing and bubbling in the film cans, Keaton and Bogart and Ambrose and cowboys and lovers and comedians and tragedians and anthropomophized animals going to hot celluloid mash and Karloff and other monsters writhing in flames a final time and Dracula turning not to dust but to ash in the light. Of Dali and Goya obliterated, of the Dutch masters erased, of Picasso and Jones, Parker and Stone, wiped out. Of books erupting from their shelves and briefly twisting, tumbling, somersaulting through the superheated air like myriad blind birds, fire snatching them down and gnawing through their hides to the soft, sweet innards, Homer, Dante, Milton, gone, Twain, Melville, Tolstoy, gone, Ferber, Porter, O'Connor, Camus, gone gone gone forever, while in the walls Beethoven and Handel and Stravinsky and Artie and Billie and Benny and Elvis and Risa and all the rest of them hit one high swift note in perfect unison and then are silent.

"You sons of bitches," I murmur through my tears. "God damn your souls to Hell, you wretched bastards...."

"Hey," one of the soldiers growls, "watch that talk. We had our orders, you saw 'em. We *had* to blow it all up."

"Had to." A numb echo. I am shaking with grief. "*Had* to blow it all up. All the literature, the paintings, sculpture, the films, the music, oh God, the best we had to give, God, God damn it. All there was that made us noble and beautiful and fine and great, and *you had to blow it up*."

"Well, hell." The lieutenant spits. "We couldn't let *them* have it, could we?"

Slices of Sylvia

Just inside the foyer, where the air was thick with dust motes and the smell of tired feet, Harris paused to check his mail box. It contained a statement from his bank and a flyer announcing super savings at a downtown department store's pre-inventory sale. No bills, at least, he thought, closing the box and locking it. No surprises.

He turned and wearily regarded the staircase. The strips of carpet that cushioned the steps were threadbare and tearing loose from the tacks. But it was no use complaining to anyone, he reflected as he placed his foot on the first step, his hand upon the smooth wooden banister. The apartment manager was always too drunk. Harris ascended slowly, counting. One. Two. The staircase seemed more treacherous each time he used it.

And, he thought grimly, each time—three—it takes me a little longer. Four. Listen to me. Panting. The going gets harder every day—five—and Gary Mitchell Harris gets older. Six. Fifty-eight years old now, my God, fifty-nine years old the month after next! How can it be? Seven. How?

He paused at the eighth step for a moment and added it up, all of it, parents, schools, pulp magazines pored over in bed on humid summer midnights, the war, coming home to Edith, the job with Platt and Sons, Edith coming out of her wedding clothes, a stillborn son, two miscarriages, Sylv—

He took another step. Nine.

Sylvia Taylor, and after Sylvia Taylor, what was it now? Ten years? *Ten?*

Ten.

Fifty-eight years, all right, and soon to be fifty-nine. Jesus. Jesus H. Christ.

Eleven.

He had almost reached the top when Ken Parker appeared on the landing and grinned down at him. Parker was an enormous man with deepset eyes. His long, muscular arms and bowed legs combined with his beetling brows to give him a simian bearing.

"H'lo," said Parker. His voice was in keeping with his appearance, a rumbling bass growl. "Hot enough for you today?"

Harris nodded and made a gesture of tired triumph as he stepped onto the landing. "One of these days," he gasped, "I'm not going to make it all the damn way up. You'll have to organize a rescue team and come down and get me."

Parker snickered. "Oh, I don't know. From what I've seen, it'll be a long time before you need *me* to get you up!"

Harris stared blankly as the man laughed uproariously. Parker leaned forward and put his face close to Harris'. "I think you been holding out on me."

A fist closed on Harris' stomach. Oh God. He gripped the balustrade rail and leaned upon it for support. Not again. His heart felt leaden. Sylvia Taylor. Sylvia Taylor. Once again reaching up out of her grave, across half a continent, across a decade. He gave Parker a helpless look as the old excuses began to well up in his throat.

"I see her," Parker said boisterously, "and then I look at *you*, and I have to wonder what it is you got that I don't." He shook his head. "Can't be money." He grinned. "No offense, but it can't be your looks, neither."

Harris felt the fist's grip on his guts loosen. It's okay, he told himself. It's not Sylvia Taylor, not this time, it's something else entirely, this idiot doesn't know a thing about it, relax. Relax. He relaxed. He cleared his throat softly.

"Come on," he said. "What're you talking about?"

"The *girl*," said Parker.

"What girl?"

"The girl who came here looking for you a while ago." Parker's forehead arranged itself into a landscape of perplexity. "You mean you don't know any redhead with a great behind and—"

Parker cupped his hands in the air, several inches out from his chest.

Harris shook his head.

"Whew. That's good. Now I don't feel so old."

"What happened?"

"Not half an hour ago," Parker said, "I'd just got in from work, and I'm drinking a beer in my room. I hear somebody knocking across the hall and take a look. And there's this broad at your door. Really a nice-looking piece, like I told you. And you know me, never pass up a chance. So I tell her you aren't home from work yet, can *I* be of some help? She asks when you'll be in, and I tell her. I ask her if I can take a message or something." The big man leered. "Never hurts to find out if you can do anything for 'em, right? So she says for me to tell you to wait for her to come back, because it's real important. Well, I just naturally thought—"

"She didn't tell you what she wants?"

"Nope."

Harris scratched his throat, puzzled. "Where'd she go?"

Parker shrugged. "Maybe I should of invited her to wait in my place."

Someone entered the foyer below. Harris leaned over the rail and saw Mrs Metzger. She fumbled a key into the lock of her mail box, took out her pre-inventory sale notice, and gave it a myopic squint before disappearing into her apartment on the ground floor. Harris straightened and moved away from the rail.

"I guess I'll find out what she wants," he said over his shoulder as he headed for his door, "when she gets back."

"Whatever it is," Parker called after him, "just remember, if you need help, I'm right across the hall."

There was a thin, sour stench in Harris' apartment. For several seconds after he had closed the door, he stood with his hand curled around the knob and sniffed curiously. Too many cigarettes. Stale

— 113 —

beer, left to go warm and flat how many nights before? He walked across the living room to the coffee table, picked up a half-empty can of beer and an overflowing ash tray, carried them into the kitchen.

The predominant odor in the kitchen was that of ripening garbage. He emptied the beer into the sink, then put the can and the cigarette butts into a grocery bag bulging with coffee grounds, grapefruit halves, potato skins. Forgot to take out the garbage, he chided himself. Always forgetting to take out the garbage. He sighed resignedly and carried out the bag.

When he had returned from the trash bin behind the building, he opened all the windows in his apartment. He washed the mismatched tableware. He hid the dirty laundry and put a fresh towel on the rack in the bathroom. He straightened the sofa cushions. He ran a fingertip across a gray-brown wall. The odor in the apartment was as bad as at had been before he carried out the garbage.

Every place I've lived, he thought, has smelled and looked the same. A bird. A songbird in a cage would be nice. And maybe some kind of plant. Flowers. Brighten up the place.

He finally sat down on the sofa and waited and stared at the day's mail on the coffee table. He never got letters any more. He had not received a personal letter in ten years. Not since Brooklyn. He added it up. Not since Edith's letter. But there had been all of those letters before that.

Dear Mr Harris, one of the letters had begun, *I read in the paper about what happened to Sylvia Taylor, then I saw you on the six o'clock news tonight and I want you to know just what I think—*

Unfair. It had been unfair of the media to single him out, unfair for him to have been named, for his picture to have been shown in newspapers, magazines, on television, for his face and name to have been identified with the Sylvia Taylor incident, for him to have suffered for all nine. *Gary,* that last letter had read, *I can't stand it any more, I'm leaving, I want a divorce, it's better this way, goodbye forever Edith.* Unfair.

Harris put a cigarette between his lips and lighted it. Tired, he thought, trying to shove the ghosts back down into the darkness. Work hard all day in this stinking heat, come home tired, smells bad in here, Jesus. He sucked on the cigarette until his lips felt as though they were blistering. Fifty-eight, Harris, going on fifty-nine. What've you got to *show* for so much time?

A faded photograph, somewhere, of Seaman Gary M. Harris, USN. Pictures of and a letter from the now ex-Mrs Gary M. Harris. A string of awful jobs and crumbling rented rooms, leading slowly inland, away from the coast and Sylvia Taylor and his name, his face, his excuses. And Sylvia Taylor herself. It always came back to Sylvia Taylor, who had cost him his job and his friends and his wife and his home and his life.

—what I think of you and the other eight gutless wonders who sat by your windows and watched as somebody sliced up Sylvia Taylor for ten minutes!!!

No, no, it wasn't that way at all, you can't call me a coward, I was Leyte and Okinawa, I....

The soft, almost tentative knock at the door repeated itself.

Harris made a sound in his throat, half-moan, half-hiss, and pushed himself to his feet. He went to the door and, placing a hand lightly upon the knob, said, "Who's there?"

"Mr Harris?" A woman's voice, muffled. "Mr Gary Harris?"

He unlocked the door and opened it a few inches. The woman standing in the hall appeared to be in her early thirties. She had a full, attractive face, hazel eyes, a wide mouth. Her reddish-brown was cut short in a becoming but no-nonsense style, and she wore a light summer jacket over a white blouse and a pleated gray skirt. She carried a large handbag.

"Who are you?" Harris said.

"My name is Vonda Rickards, and I—" She shot a nervous glance along her shoulder at the sound of a door opening across the hall. "Please, may I come in?"

Harris widened the space between the door and frame and peered past her. Ken Parker filled the doorway of his own apartment. The big man grinned and winked before stepping back and closing his door.

"That's just Parker," Harris said. "Don't mind him."

"I've met Mr Parker," the woman said in a level tone. But an angry vertical furrow appeared between her eyebrows. "May come inside? It's extremely important."

He let her into the apartment. She held her handbag like a shield as she walked across the living room to the coffee table. He watched her walk and remembered what Parker had told him. Yeah. A great behind.

"Won't you sit down?" he said, closing the door. She gingerly eased herself down into the room's one armchair.

"Can I get you something to drink? Coffee? I could make you a cup of coffee."

She gave him a quick, cool smile. "Thank you, no."

Harris stood wavering between the door and her chair. "I, uh, if you prefer, I have beer, would you like a beer?"

"No, thank you, nothing. I've just eaten." She pulled a manila envelope from her handbag and began fumbling with the metal clasp. "I didn't mean to keep you waiting, Mr Harris."

"I didn't mind the wait." He tried to smile. "At least, I don't mind the wait now."

Vonda Rickards looked at him stonily. "You'd better take a seat yourself. What I have to say is a little detailed and should come as a shock. I'm very tired, and I'd rather get this over with as quickly as possible."

Harris sat on the sofa, at the end farthest from her. She took several typewritten sheets of paper from the envelope, placed them in her lap, and folded her hands atop them.

"I'd better begin by explaining who I am. Two and a half years ago, my husband and I started work on a book about the era of senseless violence in America."

"Oh." Oh. He knew. Oh.

"It will be a fairly comprehensive volume, if it's ever finished. Speck, Whitman, Manson. The Santa Cruz murders, the sex-killings in Houston." She pretended to refer to her sheets of paper. "I say *if* because we suspended work on the book when we got to Sylvia Taylor."

He could only glare at her.

"We had wanted to talk to the people who witnessed the—"

"No!" Harris lurched to his feet and stabbed a finger in her direction. "I made the mistake of talking about it right after it happened. It's hounded me ever since. Go find the others who were there. I did the talking for all nine of us. It's their turn."

"They can't talk. Seven of them are dead now, and the eighth was last seen in Boston fourteen months ago. She could be dead now, too. My husband's trying to find her. You're the only one of the nine who's definitely still alive."

"People are always dying." He jammed a cigarette into his mouth. His hand shook as he raised the lighted match.

"When we began collecting data about the Taylor murder, we learned that seven of you had moved out of the apartment building within six months of the killing."

"We weren't the most popular tenants there after the—after it happened."

Vonda Rickards consulted her papers. "July second, the summer after the murder. The Perezes, John and Rita, the two who stayed. They were on their way to spend the holiday weekend with relatives when their car somehow left the road and exploded. August fifteenth, Eugene Browning, the man who had turned up the volume of his TV set to drown out Sylvia Taylor's screams. Killed by a hit-and-run driver. Mary Mayes was found hanging from a beam in her home in Newark on December twenty-eighth of that year. The police said suicide. They presumed a fit of guilt on her part."

Forgotten between has lips, the cigarette burned down toward its filter, and an inch of ash fell across the front of his shirt, and he stood absolutely still.

"March eighteenth," the woman went on, "one year to the day after the Taylor killing, Mary Mayes' ex-roommate, Sharon Nelson, leaped, fell, or was pushed from an eleventh-story window. May fifth, the same year, Larry Coe died in Syracuse. Another hit-and-run. Now we leap ahead four years. Coe's ex-wife Grace was found dead at her home in Atlantic City, in her bathroom. She appeared to have slipped in the tub and crushed her skull. That leaves you and Ann Neville. About a year after the killing, she broke up with her husband, who, like your wife, hadn't been at the apartment that night. We think she changed her name. We've been trying to locate her, and you, for the past year. You do know how to cover your tracks, Mr Harris."

Harris removed the dead stub of cigarette from his mouth and crushed it in an ash tray. "Ten years," he said. "A lot of people die in ten years."

"Six of the seven died within a fourteen-month period. All seven died violent deaths."

"A lot of people have fatal accidents. Or commit suicide." Harris pursed his lips for a second. "You seriously trying to tell me that the guy who killed Sylvia Taylor decided to go after the witnesses?"

She folded her hands in her lap again and shook her head slowly. "I'm serious suggesting that someone who heard about the killing may have decided to... avenge her. To punish the nine people who let her die. Someone who was more than just sickened and outraged by your apathy, cowardice, whatever you want to call it." Harris' cheeks grew hot. "A maniac, but a patient, methodical one."

"I think you're crazy," Harris said. His voice sounded strangled. "If you were so sure about all this, you'd've gone straight to the cops."

She dropped her gaze from his face. "We did."

"And they didn't believe you, huh?"

"I'm afraid they didn't."

"Well, I'm not convinced, either."

Vonda Rickards looked at him earnestly. "Even we admit we can't be one-hundred-percent certain that your life's in danger. But we're certain enough to have stopped work on the book and devoted a year to tracing you and Ann Neville."

"It sounds expensive."

"Yes. Quite expensive, Mr Harris. We even resorted to a private detective."

He let his breath escape in a sibilant rush and sat down on the arm of the sofa. High on the wall opposite him, a cockroach as fat as his little finger explored a crack in the plaster. He averted his eyes, and to the woman he said, "Why?"

She looked puzzled.

"Why've you bothered?"

"Why, to warn you, of course. Just in case we happen to be on to something."

"But why?"

Again, she looked puzzled.

"I mean," Harris said, "what's it to you if I live *or* die?"

The muscles in her jaw rippled. The furrow reappeared between her eyebrows. "What it is to us," she said in a flat, measured tone, "is that we may have uncovered seven murders. It may be eight murders by now. As long as there's that chance, as long as we may have the power to prevent another death...."

Her voice trailed off into a sigh of obvious exasperation. Clutching her bag in one hand, her papers and envelope in the other, she got to her feet. "Never mind," she said. "I've had a long, hard day on the road, I'm tired, and I'm not up to drawing any comparisons for you. I've told you what I came here to tell you, Mr Harris. Now, if you'll excuse me, I must be going."

"Maybe I should walk you to your car." Harris rose. The woman's expression was completely unfriendly. He made an apologetic gesture. "This is a rough neighborhood sometimes."

"So was the one where Sylvia Taylor died." She gave him an icy smile. "She was a great object lesson for me. I have learned how to defend myself, thank you."

She had taken several brisk steps toward the door when he stopped her with, "Any idea who the avenger is?"

Vonda Rickards paused, wheeled, and studied him for a moment before answering. "No. It could be anybody within five hundred miles of New York. It could be someone who died years ago, after Grace Coe's death. It could be someone you'll never know, never even see."

"If it's anybody at all."

"Yes." She nodded. "If. Goodbye, Mr Harris." Harris stood at the center of the living room and watched her let herself out. Almost as soon as the door had closed, he heard voices in the hall, hers and Ken Parker's. He went to the door, jerked it open, and saw the woman standing at the top of the staircase. Parker stood a few steps below her, grinning up at her.

"Nice seeing you again, Miss," Harris heard the big man say.

"Thank you," she said, "but it's Mrs, and you're blocking the stairs."

Parker grinned again and held up a six-pack of beer for her inspection. "Say, I've got, an idea—"

"A remarkable event, I'm sure." Vonda Rickards took a step downward. "Now please let me pass."

Harris walked to the balustrade and glared down at Parker. "Get out of the lady's way, Ken."

Parker tucked his six-pack under his arm and flattened himself against the wall. opposite the balustrade. His grin did not go away. The woman shot Harris an angry glance as she moved past Parker. A door opened at the far end of the hall, and Harris turned his head to see old Mr Hanes lumber into view.

Vonda Rickards screamed.

Harris jerked around just in time to see a handbag ricochet off the far wall of the foyer below, scattering pens, change, a hairbrush, a dozen odd objects. Several sheets of paper settled lazily through the air. The woman was halfway down the staircase, hugging the banister, panting curses.

Harris pushed past the dumbly gaping Parker and helped her regain her feet. "Are you okay?"

She pulled away from his hands. "I got my foot caught on a loose piece of carpet. You'd better get it fixed, before somebody around here is ki—"

She bit off her sentence and limped to the bottom of the stairs. Harris was a step behind her. She picked up her bag and began collecting her belongings. He helped her.

"I'm okay," she said at length, retrieving a coin from a dusty corner.

Harris handed her a cracked compact and a felt-tip pen.

"See how easy it'd be to have a fatal accident?"

She glared, then surveyed the foyer. "I think I've got everything." An awkward pause. "Thank you."

"I'll walk you out to your car now."

Her head came up slightly. "You needn't bother."

He opened the front door and held it open. "It's no bother at all."

Vonda Rickards' mouth compressed into a wide, tight line. She stalked past him, into the gathering dusk. Harris looked up at Ken

Parker and the old man, shrugged, and hurried through the door to the woman's side. She stopped beside a dust-coated Mazda and fumbled through her handbag. He heard the clink of keys when she withdrew her hand.

"Maybe we're all wrong," she muttered. "Maybe my husband will locate Ann Neville in Boston." She shrugged. "Tell me one thing, though."

He waited for the question, but she did not ask it as she unlocked the car and slid in behind the steering wheel. Finally, he said, "What is it?"

"How do you live with it?" She had the key in the ignition slot now. "The Perezes seemed immune to guilt. They stayed. None of the publicity disturbed them. Browning turned up his TV. But it must have affected some of you."

"Oh, yeah." He smiled bitterly. "It affected some of us, all right."

She watched him for several seconds, obviously expecting him to say more. Then: "I see. Well. Goodbye again."

"Goodbye."

He closed the door for her and stepped back and watched until the car had disappeared into the twilight. The stars were beginning to come out. Crickets were beginning to chirp in earnest. Harris thrust his hands deep into his pockets and turned to face his apartment building.

Well, he thought, well, well, how about that? Know what you should have told her, Harris? You should've told her about the war and your time on a tin can and trying to get those guys out of that turret after the kamikaze plane hit it. About the fire, the smell and screams of burning men. About how you and the others tried to get them out. How that should have made a difference to everyone ten years ago, damn it. The guys trapped in the turret were your buddies, damn it, and getting them out of there was your business. And Sylvia Taylor was just some bimbo you'd never seen or heard of before who was out at an hour and in a place she shouldn't have been....

He closed his eyes, and in the parking lot below his window the knife went into the woman's shoulder, came out black, went into her face, her neck. She collapsed screaming and pulled the man down with her. He pushed himself up on a hand and knees, and the knife kept going into her, into her, into her.

While we watched.

Harris opened his eyes as a mosquito buzzed in his ear. He jerked his head away from the sound and plodded toward the building, entered and crossed the foyer to the staircase. Ken Parker and the old man were nowhere in sight. He put his foot on the first step. One. He went up slowly, breathing hard, clutching the banister as he counted each step, two, three, wary of the ancient, treacherous carpeting. Four, five. Six. Boston, he thought. Seven. Ann Neville, he thought, and savagely kicked at a loose strip of carpet. *Eight.*

Willow Beeman

(with Howard Waldrop)

There never was another man like Willow Beeman. There never would be, either, because Willow was the very last man in the whole world. His heart was closed to the memory of men, and he did quite well without that memory, thinking of himself only as a large dog without hair.

He could recall a time, long, long before, when he had been not a dog but a gorilla, or something close to it, at any rate. But he had forgotten all the parts about being a man and living in Sumer, in Babylon and Tyre and Rome. He even disremembered about Cheyenne and Bismarck and Bayonne, and about women, cigarettes, automobiles, ice cream, God, spaceships, books, and underarm deodorants. He would not even have remembered being a gorilla were it not for his friend Patrox, who was something very like a Galapagos tortoise and had lived quite a long time. "Longer than you, anyway," Patrox was fond of reminding Willow.

Patrox was also fond of telling stories. Willow found these stories disturbing. They were full of esoteric references that got into his skull and nibbled at his brains. "What is *suburb?*" Willow would demand, seizing upon an odd word in one of Patrox's incomprehensible yarns, and Patrox would shrug and say that he didn't really know. "Then why do you tell these stories?" Willow would ask, and Patrox would shrug again and say that he didn't really know that, either. "I think you're making it all up," Willow would declare, by way of closing the subject, and stomp away in a sulk, irritated as all get-out by the nibbling going on in his head.

Willow Beeman was not singular in his disbelief in both men and his own man-ness. Once he had cast off the memories, to say nothing of the overbearing swaggers, of *Homo sapiens*, it was easy for the animals to take his presence among them for granted. And, excepting Patrox, who had his doubts, they, too, thought of Willow only as a large dog without hair. Willow drank with them at the water holes and licked salt with them at the salt lick. He slept on the ground when he was tired, and he ate crawdads and wild berries when he was hungry. So he had all of the animal comforts and pleasures.

Except one. Willow kept noticing animals copulating.

"What makes them do that?" he wondered aloud one mellow day of a mellow spring.

"There's a story about it," Patrox murmured at his side. "But it's a dirty one, and my mother would spin in her grave if I told it."

Willow frowned, perplexed by the oddness of the words *dirty* and *grave*. His head began to throb from the nibbling. He turned Patrox over onto his shell and left him kicking there for a day or two, just to pay him back.

As the mellow spring passed into a mellower summer, Willow noted that all of the animals who had previously been copulating were now birthing lots of little animals which resembled them somewhat, despite a certain largeness of skull and a marked clumsiness of foot. Willow devoted no small amount of thought to the matter and, by and by, put together a fantastic theory, which he then presented to Patrox.

Patrox listened, nodded sagely, and said, "See, Willow, I told you it was dirty."

"You mean, I'm right?" said Willow, awed by his own hitherto unsuspected brilliance.

"You hit the nail squarely on the head," Patrox affirmed.

Willow winced and rubbed his temples.

A little more time passed, and Willow Beeman forgot all of his newly gained knowledge of reproduction. Or, rather, he placed the information in that portion of his mind which contained all the rest of the useless information he had accumulated about the way the world was. Like how the leaves kept coming off the trees at a certain time of year. Like how that big useless white thing in the night skies sometimes was round and sometimes was only a curved line of light with pointy ends and sometimes was not there at all.

But another mellow spring came along eventually, and Willow looked around at the copulating animals, sighed, sat down on Patrox's back, and said, "I'm lonely. I think."

"You have me, don't you?" said Patrox.

"Well, it occurs to me that this thing the animals do must be a lot of fun, since all of the animals do it at least once a year. And they always seem to be in great spirits afterward.

"How well I remember!" Patrox snorted. There was a note of longing in his snort.

"Really, Patrox? You've done it, too?"

"Yes, but it was a long time ago, when I was young and limber and full of juice, so don't get any ideas. Besides, we're both boys."

"What's *boys*?"

"Never mind, Willow."

Willow ground his teeth in frustration for a few seconds. Then: "Patrox, the more I think about it, the more I'd like to have some little animals that look like me. So I'm just going to have to find somebody with whom to do this wonderful copulation thing."

And he did, too.

It took Willow Beeman five weeks to recover completely from the wounds he suffered at the claws of the she-wolverine. He wondered where he had gone wrong.

"As I remember it," Patrox told him, "animals only copulate with other animals of the same kind."

"I'll have to find another big, hairless dog in that case," said Willow. Or, he added to himself, if that doesn't pan out, at least a gorilla.

"I tend to doubt that you'll find another big, hairless dog out here in the woods, Willow."

"Maybe I should go to one of those places that don't look like the woods," and, six days later, Willow pulled into just such a place. It was actually all that was left of a city, but Willow didn't know this. He was rather sore of foot and had begun to ache peculiarly in the groin, which is how it goes when notions about copulation take root in one's brains. Willow searched through the city, looking at disintegrating hulks of automobiles, rust-eaten shards of tin cans, a Lacrosse missile launcher, and the like, though, to Willow, these things were just some sort of strange plant life that couldn't be eaten.

Willow began to lose heart after a while. "This isn't getting me anywhere," he muttered to himself. "I do believe I've been everywhere in this place, and I haven't seen a single dog. Or even any gorillas. Maybe it'd be better if I just went on back to the woods and spent my time crawfishing with my hands in some pool."

It was as he was about to leave the place that he came upon the low stone edifice with its door ajar and the sign that read cryogen, inc. Willow couldn't read the sign, reading being one of the things Patrox had never quite got around to showing him how to do. But the door was half-open, and Willow, who was now feeling rather ferocious with frustration, barged in furiously. What happened next you would not believe, even if we told you. Suffice it for explanation that there was still some power running this or that arcane machine when Willow entered.

Willow stayed inside for a long, *long* time. When this or that arcane machine finally did sputter and give up the ghost, thereby releasing Willow from his protracted sleep, the low stone edifice had been worn away to the level of the ground. The door and the sign were gone, too.

Willow sat up, looked around, and immediately saw that the strange, inedible plant life had given way to salt marshes and mud flats. There were a few stunted, scraggly trees, several of whom regarded him with baleful equivalents of eyes. Their attitude toward him appeared to be, "Hmpf, and what is *this?*"

Willow scratched his skull bemusedly and asked, "Where've all the animals gotten off to?"

"Dead and gone, most of them!" snapped one of the trees. "And good riddance, I say!"

Willow recalled the purpose in his coming to the place. "You haven't seen any big, hairless dogs around here, have you? Or any gorillas?"

"No dogs or gorillas," the tree answered irritably. "Just something that looks very like a Galapagos tortoise."

"That must be Patrox!"

"Yes, I believe he did say his name was Patrox. And, now that I think about it, he spoke of some animal that looks the way you look. He said that he had known this animal a long time ago and had always thought highly of it." The tree peered closely at Willow. "I can't say as I find much in you to think highly of."

Willow was dejectedly surveying the new landscape. "So everything is gone," he muttered.

"What did you expect?" the tree demanded. "I've been listening to your infernal snoring ever since I can remember, and my mother says you were here when *she* was a sapling. You've been asleep for some time, and things have a natural tendency to change with time. Even people, though they generally resist that change."

"What is *people?*"

"Why, now that most of the animals are gone, people are the dominant form of life on the Earth today. Look, I can't stand here all day and explain things to you, so why don't you walk around and sort of acclimate yourself to stuff. It stands to reason that you've got some catching up to do."

"What is *reason?*"

"Never you mind. Now run along."

Willow Beeman ran along, still considerably confounded. The world seemed drabber, uglier. The air tasted funny. Frankly, Willow was fairly well put out with it all after he had acclimated himself to only a few square miles of stuff. He parked his fanny on a smooth, green rock and said, "On top of everything else, I still haven't gotten to do what the animals do to make little animals like themselves."

"Eh?" said the rock, who was actually Patrox, who had been taking a nap. "Why, Willow! It's you! Long time, no see."

"I'm mighty glad to see you again," Willow confessed.

"Need help?" Patrox said solicitously.

"What is *help?*"

"What do you want more than anything else right now?"

"I want to copulate," said Willow. "I want to make little animals like myself. I came looking for another big, hairless dog. Or a gorilla, if I couldn't find a dog. I never found either. There must be something with which I can copulate."

"Have you tried it with people?"

"I wouldn't know people if I saw one."

Patrox squinted toward the salt marshes. "People hang around over there. As long as you're determined to do this, you might as well give them a try, Willow."

"Well, if you say so." Frowning deeply, Willow went over to the salt marshes. He returned shortly, and he was frowning more deeply than before. "They're *frogs*, Patrox. I know frogs when I see them."

"They're people now."

"But when I lived in the woods, they used to keep me awake at night going breedeep breedeep breedeep. They're frogs."

"They're the best I can offer," Patrox stated flatly. "Take them or leave them."

"Oh, all right." Willow walked back to the salt marsh and tried to get the frogs to copulate with him, but whenever he made a lunge at one of them, it would vanish in a puff of pale blue smoke.

Not like frogs at all, Willow thought disgustedly. He squatted in the muck, feeling very sorry for himself. The ache in his groin was worse now, his stomach was rumbling with hunger, and his throat was raw with thirst. He did not look up when Patrox settled into the mud at his side.

"What now?" Patrox said softly.

"I don't know," admitted Willow. "I was doing just fine in the woods. But now everything's so depressing. Where'd all the grass and ferns go? Where are the birds and deer and wolverines? I miss them. Everything's been a mess ever since I decided to make little animals like myself."

"Well, maybe that's *why* everything got messed up," Patrox said. "Weren't you happy being a big, hairless dog in the woods?"

Willow nodded forlornly.

"You probably could've gone right on being a big, hairless dog if you hadn't gone off looking for someone like yourself. When the time came for all the dogs to go away, you would simply have become something else. An ostrich, maybe. You'd have been an ostrich for as long as you could, then something else, then something else again. That's how you managed to hang on as long as you did back there in the woods, Willow."

"I'm not sure I quite follow you," Willow said, "and, besides, what's this got to do with everything going away?"

"It has everything to do with it," Patrox said. "Willow, I've always been pretty certain that you were a gorilla before you were a dog, even though I didn't know you personally before then. You yourself apparently suspect as much. Before you were a gorilla, who knows? At any rate, the point is that you, being the only one left of your kind, managed to stay alive by not being whatever it is that you really are. And as long as there was only one of you, Mother Nature could pretend not to notice you and go along with the idea of you being a gorilla or a dog or, whatever."

"But then," Patrox continued, "Mother Nature got panicky when you decided to try and make little animals like yourself. Don't you see? You were safe in the woods as long as you were content to remain one of a kind, a unique exception to the rules. If you wanted to be a gorilla, fine, Mother Nature let you be a gorilla for as long as there were real gorillas in the world. The same goes for dogs. But there just wasn't—and isn't—a place for more than a single Willow Beeman creature. While you were away, Mother Nature was making everything become extinct. She was looking for you, trying to keep you from upsetting her apple cart, but she couldn't find you. The more she didn't find you, the more panicky she became, and the more things she made become extinct. So now just about everything is gone, except for the trees and the people—and my kind. And you're in terrible danger, Willow. I suggest that you decide, but fast, what you intend to become now. You can't stay a dog, because there aren't any dogs left. You're too soft to make a good tree, even if they'd have you. And the people don't seem to care for you at all."

Patrox got to his four feet, turned, and started to amble away. "Be something quicky," he said over his shoulder. "Otherwise, Willow, you're extinct."

"But what else is there to be," Willow called after him, "if not a tree or a people?"

Patrox paused and shrugged within his shell.

Willow Beeman got up out of the muck and walked over to him. "Say, Patrox, why don't I be whatever you are?"

Patrox laughed. "Now *that* would be interesting. But what would you do for a shell? Your camoflauge has to be good if you don't want to die off."

"I—I could make a shell out of dried mud." Willow walked around Patrox several times, examining him closely. "Yes, I think it can be done. I'll be one of your kind. Uh, Patrox? Just what *are* you, anyway. I mean, in case anybody asks."

"Don't you think that I look very like a Galapagos tortoise" Patrox inquired slyly.

"But what are you *really?*"

Patrox looked around and asked, in a lowered voice, "You promise you won't ever tell anyone?"

"I promise, Patrox," said Willow.

"Tyrannosaurus rex, at your service, Willow."

Haiti

Miami was coming in so strong and clear that it fairly blasted me awake. Usually, you couldn't get it at all. Every once in a great while, atmospherics would bounce it right to my bedside. The signal would arrive so winded and shivery from its run down the Cuba-Bahama gantlet that feeble, sputtery Radio Soleil could bully it to extinction. But not today. Today, the news was that the U.S. expedition to Mars had finally reached its destination. You had to figure that Miami would boost its signal for something like that. You had to wonder what the Cubans were making of it as they huddled in their caves. Another *yanqui* stunt, probably.

I looked across the room at Velmont, who was sitting on the edge of his iron-frame bed, one sock on and one sock off. He seemed to be having trouble remembering whether he was supposed to be dressing or undressing. He reached a decision after a moment, took the one sock off, unbuttoned his shirt, began removing items from various pockets and placing them on the night table.

"Bad night?" I said.

He grunted noncommittally. "You're running late."

"We take you now to the White House," said the voice from the radio, "where the president is about to—"

"You're right," I said to Velmont, and switched the radio off. "How's our cholera patient?"

"Died in the night."

I watched him do a slow-motion keel-over. He must've been asleep the instant his head touched his pillow. Quietly but quickly, I got up, washed, dressed. He was snoring softly when I left the room.

Our quarters occupied half the second floor of a long, narrow building that served as the rear wall of a courtyard behind the hospital building. The other boundaries of the yard were defined by sheds housing Dr de Rossarieu's van on one side and the kitchen and the laundry on the other; a strong gate and some unattractive sections of wall, built of cinder blocks and odd pieces of brick, had been erected in the gaps. Marie met me at the kitchen door with my breakfast, black coffee, hot bread, a piece of fruit. I took it into the hospital and ate in what we called the doctors' lounge, a corner separated from the ward by a rickety wooden partition.

De Rossarieu came in, red-eyed and uncombed. His clothes looked as if he'd slept in them, though he probably hadn't got more than fifteen minutes of sleep at a stretch during the past two or three days. Come my own bedtime, I slept hard; only that old cheap clock radio could rouse me any more. Depending upon how things were going with us otherwise, I thought de Rossarieu was either a remarkable human dynamo or else a mere crazy insomniac. Either way, he could be worrisome.

By way of greeting, he said, in French, "Our cholera patient died in the night."

"Velmont told me."

"Not an hour ago, a mother brought in her child with the same blue coloration. She said she believed there are many more sick people, especially in Cité Carton." My heart sank when he mentioned Cité Carton, poorest part of Cité Soleil, poorest slum in Port-au-Prince, poorest city in the Americas. "Telephone service is limited this morning. I have already alerted the clinics and the Baptist mission, but not the Schweitzer. Not that anyone will have supplies to spare if we need them, but we must all be ready to meet this emergency."

I said, like a fool, "What about the mayor, the government?"

"The mayor appears not to have telephone service this morning. Perhaps we have no mayor this morning. I did talk to a

Monsieur Lodeon, who evidently is the new public works minister. He understands the importance of locating the source of infection and has promised to find out which public pumps are in operation. One of the clinics is sending people to do the testing."

He paused for such a long time that I said, "Does that exhaust the government's resources?"

"I have also talked to someone at the health ministry," he said, "or whatever passes for it now. A Monsieur Bazile."

"And?"

"Perhaps, perhaps. He promised to give the matter personal attention."

We both knew how much we could depend on promises. We'd just have to do the best we could. Health-care providers in our situation had just had to do the best they could ever since the collapse of the World Health Organization. That old network was long gone, and there was no new network worthy of the name. We were nearly out of everything, bedspace, antibiotics, money, options. So was everybody else. Cholera control in the Caribbean was returning to the sorry state it'd been in before the first International Sanitary Conference in the 1890s.

De Rossarieu fastened a sorrowful eye on me and said, "We have to know how bad it is in our quarter. You must go to Cité Carton this morning. Take Georges with you. He can interpret for you. Creole sounds very strange when you speak it."

I barely heard the last part. My heart had sunk through the floor. Cité Carton!

"Velmont's a local boy," I said, "why not send him?" I instantly regretted my words. They made me sound like a slacker, a soft sluggish whining white boy.

The doctor didn't reproach me, didn't, in fact, seem to mind the question at all. Still, his reply made me feel as if I had all the staying power of milk set in the hot sun. "Velmont has had a hard night," he said, "and needs his rest, and we can't wait even a few hours while he gets it. Two cases in the ward could mean hundreds, thousands, of cases out there. We have to know. We have to convince people to bring in anyone with cholera symptoms."

And not, I thought bitterly, anyone with the symptoms of one of the half dozen other sanitation-related diseases that're always loose in Cité Carton.

"I think," he said, "the people have lost faith in us. Fewer and fewer come in for checkups—"

He stopped abruptly. His expression sagged. We operated under the auspices of the Medical Social Complex of Cité Soleil, which had begun over half a century before with a single clinic and gradually expanded to several more clinics and curative hospitals. We stressed preventive care. Four times a year, sick or not, everyone got a free checkup. As simple a system as that had cut the local infant-mortality rate from almost one in four to less than one in ten—as much of a miracle as anyone could've hoped to work here. Still, human miracles cost money, and not much of that had been forthcoming lately. We were losing more babies, one in eight, losing ground, one in seven, almost one in six. You had to wonder what the ones who were being saved were being saved for. AIDS? Tuberculosis?

I looked out into the ward and saw Nurse Siniamen and one of our Catholic Daughters of Charity moving about among the beds. The hospital had been a warehouse before its conversion. Beds, some screened, lined the walls, and there was a big square-angled archipelago of them in the center of the room. Everything had been put in with regard for efficient use of space. Yet it all looked like everything else in the country, tossed together, falling apart.

"We won't be able to take care of a dozen cholera patients," I said, "let alone hundreds or thousands."

De Rossarieu made no reply. He looked stuporous, looked stricken, and after a moment I thought, suddenly, clearly, and terrifiedly, Is he having a *stroke?* After a moment more, he shook off what was, after all, only a daze of exhaustion and started talking again, muttering to himself, "And how can we *blame* them for not coming in? Without medicines, equipment, we cannot help them. Without our help, they sicken and die..."

De Rossarieu may have been a human dynamo, but he was an aging one, fifty-five, sixty years old if he was a day. Trying to save the world was going to drop him dead in his tracks one day, but first not being able to save the world was going to make him crazy. I put my hand on his arm, spoke his name sharply, watched him return to me, the hospital, his own body. He couldn't sleep and wouldn't use drugs. At the moment, he wasn't in any shape to treat hangnail, never mind cholera. I wished I could've ordered him to get some sleep, or else had the nerve to slip him a sleeping pill. That I would have to do on my own. Hardworking and efficient Nurse Siniamen would sooner have kissed a *fer-de-lance* than betray or defy him. She worshipped him, maybe loved him, and didn't care much for me at all. The rest of the day staff consisted of two Catholic Daughters of Charity. The place was relatively understaffed at night, with only Velmont and another Daughter in the ward, though de Rossarieu, the nurse, and I were always close by. This was Haiti. You just had to do the best you could.

I left the doctor in the lounge and made a quick circuit of the ward to let Nurse Siniamen know what was going on. Georges was helping his mother in the kitchen shed. He was twelve years old, tall for his age, wiry, quiet, and thoroughly Haitian in his attitude toward unpleasant work. It had to be done if it had to be done. I asked Marie to let me borrow him for a few hours. She clicked her tongue dismayedly when I mentioned Cité Carton but gave her permission. Georges just said, "Okay," a word he liked a lot.

I couldn't think of many worse ways to begin the day than with a stroll through a slum. A stroll it would be, too. The hospital had only one motor vehicle, de Rossarieu's ancient, smoky van, which we used, whenever we had precious gasoline, as an ambulance or to haul medical supplies. Not that there often were medical supplies. We had several bicycles, but even if I'd felt like risking my own— it was probably the most valuable possession I had at hand, and surely a temptation to some individuals—it would've been useless where I was going. There were no streets there, only crooked paths. Because of the rains, the ground would have the consistency of custard.

Nurse Siniamen helped the boy and me adjust the straps of our packs. She didn't say goodbye or wish us luck or anything, merely nodded wordlessly. After three years, she remained very conscious of my race and my nationality and probably believed I was a spy.

Haitians had little cause to trust United Stateseans, who, after all, had spent over a hundred years mucking around here, until the place was finally, completely, irreversibly mucked up. Not that it had all been the fault of the U.S. government and U.S. business, not by a long shot: the Duvaliers and Bonne and the rest of those monsters had all been homeboys; King Henri Christophe had set the pattern in the early 1800s. Georges and I went out a side door. The morning was cool, for Haiti, and humid, laced with the fumes of fires and carrying a hint of ripened garbage from the direction of the harbor.

You couldn't see both sides of the street for people. You almost couldn't move forward, either, if you were going against the current. No crowd anywhere in the world, not in Hong Kong, Tokyo, Mexico City, Calcutta, can be denser than a Port-au-Prince crowd. We were headed toward the muddy plain on which the slums festered. Traffic tried to turn us around and carry us back as it flowed from the worst parts of Cité Soleil through the less-bad parts—no part deserved to be called a good part. By comparison, downtown Port-au-Prince looked prosperous, as long as you didn't look too closely at the sad, tired Victorian structures and the pocked streets. Caribbean markets are, traditionally, crowded and noisy places where the lure of commerce was irresistible, but here it was strictly subsistence commerce, and the noise is less exuberant than desperate. Once, I'd read, Port-au-Prince was full of beggars. No more. There was no one to beg from.

The boy easily kept pace at my side. Just before the street curved sharply, I paused and looked back. The hospital sat like a squat blue bluff above a restless river of dark faces, scarves, wide-brimmed straw hats. Those familiar blue walls housed the only thing like a home I had in Haiti. There were hills behind the city, and mountains behind the hills. Centuries of unhappy Haitian history were compressed in a single local proverb, *Dèyè morne ginyin morne*, "Beyond the mountains, more mountains."

We got through the market-place mob without incident and left pavement behind. The muddy road narrowed and began to braid like a lazy old river. Soon enough, we faced a daunting maze of slippery filth-strewn paths. Cité Carton was built on landfill. The houses, if they could be dignified with that word, were fashioned of scraps of corrugated tin, scraps of wood, cardboard—thus, City of Cartons. The boundary of a yard might be marked with a few sticks driven into the ground. There was no potable water, no sewerage system. The ground was squishy, putrid jam. You didn't want to breathe through your nose, because the stench of human and animal waste was unbearable. You didn't want to breathe through your mouth, because flies were everywhere. You didn't want to breathe at all.

Adults looked at us—at me, really—with suspicion in their expressions, or with frank hostility, or with nothing at all. The children, all showing signs of severe malnutrition, reddish hair, distended bellies, looked curious or alarmed or, most depressingly, as devoid and incapable of emotion as some of the adults. When I decided we had come far enough, I slipped off my pack and slowly executed a 360-degree turn, so that everyone could see the big caduceus printed on the front of my T-shirt. I announced, in French, that I was from the Medical Social Complex hospital, gave my name, and told them why I had come. Georges waited until I was finished, then translated. No one appeared to find me very impressive. Then one small girl, ten, maybe twelve years old, beckoned urgently from around the corner of a hut. As I approached, she pointed to the open doorway. I stuck my head inside.

The hut consisted of a single room, about three meters to a side, with shaky walls of corrugated sheet tin and cardboard. In somebody's mind, a filmy sheet of plastic hanging against one wall turned what otherwise would've been only a hole into a legitimate window. Stacked against the rear wall were several flattened cardboard boxes covered with what must've appeared to be cabalistic markings to anybody who couldn't read, which was nine Haitians in ten—no hook, 1 doz, c/#: 318, 7875/20, 3-2-31, made in korea. In one corner, a small black cooking pot sat by a cold hearth made of stones and bits of cinder block. Some grimy plastic sandals in children's sizes were piled in the opposite corner. A sheet of cardboard was on the ground in the center of the room, and on the cardboard was a naked boy about four years old. His eyes and cheeks were sunken, his lips were bluish, and he was cold and clammy to the touch. He lay unconscious in a light-gray scum of his own watery stools. Even in Cité Carton, with its perennial dense fecal miasma, there must've been smells you could get used to, but cholera couldn't have been one of them.

The girl hovered in the doorway. I said, in Creole, "Is this your brother? Where are your mother and the rest of your family?" She looked puzzled, so I had Georges repeat what I'd said. He rattled it off like a machine gun. The girl tried to squirm away from the questions.

I heard a blur of voices from without. The girl suddenly vanished from the doorway, and Georges made an alarmed sound and glanced back over his shoulder at me. He looked sick with fear. I came out of the hut to find myself facing a solid line of sullen grown-ups. Georges stepped to my side, and I drew him behind me.

A withered old man dressed in a ratty suit a size too small for him said, in uncertain French, "Now you see everyone is sick, go away."

"I am from the hospital," I said.

"*I* am the doctor here," said the old man, "ever since the *loa* mounted me as I was a boy—" he grinned horribly at Georges, who was peeking around me "—like this one." He meant that he was the *houngan*, possessed by one of the wise old voodoo gods. You couldn't live in this country without hearing such stuff. "You do no good here. Go back," and he nodded toward the distant hills.

I looked him straight in the eye and said, "There is a child sick with cholera here. There have been two other cases since yesterday. Many people are going to die here if—"

"Many people always die here. It is because the people abandoned the *loas*. The *loas* send punishments. Go away now. Your medicine, nothing you have works here any longer."

"I have come from the hospital to learn how many people are sick here." I made myself speak calmly but earnestly and tried to project purposefulness, self-confidence, but not arrogance. "I have to know where you are getting your drinking water now."

"Everything is different now," said the *houngan*. "You have no power to help, or to stay."

Him I could have argued with all day, but not the machetes I suddenly noticed in the hands of several of the men standing with him. The *houngan* had already put me in my place; I had no authority here; these people looked perfectly willing to chop me down in broad daylight if I persisted. I indicated surrender with a nod, turned Georges and myself around, started us walking back the way we'd come. It wasn't until I had taken six or seven steps that I truly stopped expecting a blade to bite into the side of my neck. The fact remained that I was being shown out under guard. I did what tradition and history dictated, kept my manly head up, my noble gaze fixed on the horizon, fought the need to start crying from anger, frustration, and humiliation. Just like Lee at Appomattox.

No one threw anything harder than catcalls, but our escort stayed with us until our feet struck hard, rough pavement. Then the men stood around to watch us go and make sure we didn't sneak back. The *houngan* gave me a grin of pure hateful triumph. The girl who had summoned me to her baby brother's side called after us, softly, "*Bonsoir*," and started to wave, but someone struck her hand down.

It was a hot, grim slog back. Georges wasn't a talkative lad, and I wasn't in a talky mood, and just as well. He'd have got a complete education in swearing in English, and later his mother, who feared only God, would've repaid me with a complete education in bawling out in Creole and French. Those are fine languages for bawling out, but when you feel the need to capture the gist of a intolerable situation in a few words, or to sum up the character, ancestry, and destiny of some vile ignorant lowdown awful-smelling dog-kicking snake-sucking soft-brained syphilitic sack of skunk pus *voodoo doctor*, you can't beat the old Anglo-Saxonisms for savor.

Then I found myself thinking, not for the first or tenth or forty-seventh time, that three years' worth of my energy and ability was a respectable contribution, I could retire with honor intact now, go back to the U.S. of A., patch up things with my family somehow, start making something like a good living and living something like the good life. You could make yourself crazy this way. Lord knows, I'd never had any illusions about Haiti, but your usual run of idealistic young idiot, once having alienated great Doctor Dad and broken great Doctor Mom's heart by becoming a *physician's assistant*—not even a general practitioner!—would be satisfied to spend a year in one of the States' numerous, varied, and worsening hell-holes before moving on to a more genteel practice. Yours truly, however, had wanted, not a *job* in some piss-ant emergency room in the current murder capital of the U.S., but A Real Challenge, by God, nothing less than, nowhere else but, *the* hell-hole of the Western Hemisphere.

Great Doctor Mom had begun her last letter to me, *My Dear Son, The world will, eventually, break your heart.* In that same letter, she told me that she'd wired what she called my "mad money" to the American embassy in Port-au-Prince. *I'd sooner throw money down the toilet,* she wrote, *than put it in Haitian banks. You can withdraw it any time you feel you've had enough and are ready to come home and lead a real life.*

The money was still at the embassy. I thought about it as little as possible. You could make yourself crazy.

We got back to the hospital shortly after two o'clock in the afternoon. I was bone-tired, footsore, and mad enough to punch an archbishop. De Rossarieu had managed to get to sleep for about twenty minutes at midday. It left him looking a bit less red-eyed but even more uncombed. When I finished describing my visit to and ejection from Cité Carton, he said, "It is worse than I feared. But I do have some good news. Monsieur Bazile from the health ministry has made an appointment for this afternoon. I need you to go." I stifled a groan. More legwork. "Bazile thinks our only hope of getting medical supplies is to get them from the United States."

"The United States," I said, annoyedly lapsing into English, "is why we don't have what we need in the first place."

De Rossarieu understood English perfectly well and followed my lead. "Bazile thinks now is psychologically the right moment. The Americans are in a good mood about this Mars landing, and the war in Cuba seems to be going well for them."

"Well, that tells you about U.S. priorities. I don't think we can get squat. They don't even have airbases here. They fly all their missions out of Florida and Santo Domingo. Christ, I don't even think they have an ambassador here."

"They have an embassy and a *chargé*, at least. If I have to use my one American staff member to pry help out of the American embassy...."

"You're right." Of course he was right. "Where's this meeting supposed to take place?"

"In Independence Square. The health minister will meet you there himself."

"I don't like that one bit," I said. "Shouldn't a legitimate health ministry have a real *office* somewhere?"

De Rossarieu heaved a great sigh. "What in Haiti is legitimate any more? Maybe he keeps his office in his hat."

An hour later, scrubbed clean of Cité Carton muck, dressed in my one decent suit of clothes, and still bone-tired and footsore, I set out on my bicycle for Independence Square. I pedaled part of the way, pushed the bike the rest. The going was slow; long stretches of pavement had disintegrated into a detritus of asphalt and gravel. The crowd had thinned away almost to nothing by the time I reached the plaza and sat down across from the statue of Toussaint L'Ouverture, hero of the 1791–1803 war for independence from France. Significantly, I thought, he had his back turned to the National Palace.

For the first time all day, for the first time in many days, I felt I was breathing relatively clean air. But of course. Here, as elsewhere, relatively clean air had become a commodity, and breathing it, a privilege of those who could afford it. The hills above the city were given over to upper-class suburbs, Pètionville and the like, now mostly, albeit unofficially, deserted. There was nothing left to plunder in Haiti, so there were no plunderers left, either—none who'd been good at it, anyway. With car doors locked, windows rolled up, eyes looking straight ahead, the last rich Haitian aristocrats had driven their expensive automobiles to the airport a final time and escaped to the south of France. The last poor Haitian aristocrats hung on meanly in their hillside palaces—you never saw them anywhere any more, or soldiers, uniformed policemen, or government officials, for that matter. From time to time, you heard somebody's name mentioned after the phrase "President of the Republic of Haiti" on the radio, saw a name after that title in some inconsequential newspaper story, but no one could tell you who he was, what he looked like, how much harm he was doing to the country.

No government, colonial, monarchical, democratic, dictatorial, had ever done Haiti any good. I had only to look around the plaza, the so-called Champs de Mars, to see signs of national dissolution. The National Palace was a lifeless pile of masonry with a forlorn air about it, a look of having been abandoned to ghosts. I could see windows with glass broken out, either by winds or vandals. Grass was growing through cracks in the pavement. The building looked as haunted as Sans Souci, old King Henri's palace in the north, built in 1813. I'd seen that on one of my few trips into the countryside. Except for Sans Souci and King Henri's nearby fortress, La Citadelle, and maybe a picturesque fishing village or two, there weren't lots of what you could call tourist attractions anywhere in Haiti. There was no woodland any more. Halfhearted reforestation efforts in the late twentieth century came to nothing; poor country folk, needful of fuel for cooking fires, cut down the trees faster than they could be replaced. Without the trees, erosion was widespread and rapid. Haitian rivers were vicious torrents. The whole western end of the island of Hispaniola was being washed into the sea. Almost the whole population of Haiti had already been washed into the slums of Port-au-Prince. This had been the richest colony in the world in the eighteenth century.

A once-elegant automobile came around the square and crept to a stop not far from where I sat. Both front doors opened, and out stepped two men wearing what had come down from the days of the old Tontons Macoute as the official badge of bogeymanhood, dark sunglasses. The driver stepped forward and asked my name. I told him. He was wearing a blue serge suit and an open-necked shirt and had a pistol stuck conspicuously in the waistband of his trousers. He said almost in English, "I mass fris you." He ran his hands under my jacket, up my sides, knelt to feel along each leg from hip to ankle, stood up, stepped back, nodded. The whole procedure had taken four, five seconds. He took my bicycle around to the back of the car and stowed it in the trunk. His gaunt fellow bogeyman, looking like some cheap clothes filled with bones, opened a rear door for me. I started to get in. A heavyset man sat waiting in the back seat.

I hesitated. "Monsieur Bazile?"

"Of course." He spoke heavily accented English.

"From the health ministry?" I hoped against hope that there'd been some mistake. Bazile and his car and his two bogeymen looked about as official as a sawed-off shotgun.

"Of course. Come, get in." I got in, and the car started to move. Bazile cocked his head slightly and seemed to listen to the motor for a second or two. Then he smiled at me.

"Doctor de Rossarieu," he said, "told me you have personally investigated the situation."

"I'm afraid it wasn't much of an investigation. The local *houngan* showed me out."

"Ah! The *loas* are here to stay! The Holy Church could not drive them out. Not even Bonne's New Haitian Order could do that." His smile got slier. "Not even your marines could do it."

"Knocking off Trinidad and Tobago is more the marines' speed." Lately, "my" marines, along with the rest of "my" armed forces, had been using Cuba for a target range.

"The American military," said Bazile, "may be our salvation. The American base at Santo Domingo will have the medical supplies we need. I have already been in touch with the *chargé d'affaires* at your embassy and he has cabled Washington."

I gave him a tight smile. "It's no embassy of mine."

"Do you dislike your own countrymen?"

"These particular countrymen always look like they were carved out of brie."

That obviously made no sense whatever to him. I opened my mouth to offer some sort of explanation, but he said, "You are a young and impatient man." His voice became conspiratorial. "Suffer these embassy people for a while, my friend. Transfers of money and medical supplies present everyone with certain opportunities."

I stared at him. He became seriously preoccupied with the back of his driver's head. We rode in silence for a time, then turned onto the driveway of a mansion.

Bazile smiled as his men got out to open the doors for us. Disgruntled, I said, "Nice place you have here."

His smile widened into a grin. "Oh, no, this is one of the houses kept by the American foreign-service people."

"Don't they have a compound any more?"

"Only the marines stay there now," he said. "It isn't nearly as nice as this. If you are thinking of buying a home in Haiti, now is the time."

"You wouldn't by any chance be in the real-estate business, would you?"

"I am in every kind of business there is."

I'll bet, I thought.

Inside, the place had a half moved-into or -out-of look, but it was cool and pleasant-smelling. Waiting to receive us there were two creatures from another world, male and female. The lightness of their skin and hair was offset by dark clothing; their pale, almost translucent faces and hands seemed to shimmer. I couldn't imagine their having ever been out in the Haitian sun, and wondered what they might do if they were exposed to it. Crumble like Dracula, maybe, flake away to nothing. Maybe melt like cheese. I'd never seen these people before, and yet I had. They could've been clones of everyone who'd worked at the embassy before them. Bazile made the introductions. The man, Fraser, was the *chargé*. The woman's name was Britton. No one bothered to say what her job was; she could have been the embassy secretary or Fraser's lady friend.

Bazile was expansive. "I have heard it on the radio!" he gushed to Fraser. "Americans on Mars! It is a magnificent accomplishment! You must be very proud of your countrymen!"

Fraser beamed as if his brains and his personal fortune were responsible for the feat. Britton said, "Yes, very proud." Before I could draw a breath to mention cholera, Fraser suggested that we go see if there were anything new about the landing on television, and the four of us drifted into a sitting room.

What I'd always called the approved-news channel was running videotape from Mars. Bazile and the two embassy people were enthralled. I fretted and waited for the right instant to bring them down to earth.

"Still," Bazile said, "it strikes me as most strange to send men all that way to Mars with only other men to look at and talk to for so long."

"Maybe they're all homos up there," I growled.

Everybody looked at me in surprise.

"The president hates homos," I said. "Heard him say so in a speech. Probably spend billions to send all those HIV-positives someplace faraway. Maybe even to Mars."

Fraser and Britton were becoming unhappier with me by the second, but Bazile evidently decided that this was authentic American humor, the fabled leg-pulling variety, for he threw back his head and gave a hearty laugh.

"Still," he said, dabbing at a tear of mirth with one thick finger, "it cannot be cost-effective." He lowered his hand from his face and cocked his thumb; his finger became the barrel of a gun. "There are less expensive ways of dealing with the problem."

I thought that this might be authentic bogeyman humor, the leg-breaking kind, so I chuckled appreciatively. Then I said, "Now that we've all seen Mars and shared a laugh or two, let's talk about a problem brewing in the Cité Carton section of Cité Soleil."

"Ah!" said Bazile. "That terrible place! But when has it not been so?"

"There're people sick with cholera there," I said, "and I can't get near them. I got chased out this morning by a witch doctor and some boys with machetes."

"Chased out of the slums, for Heaven's sake," said Britton.

"One of those sanitation-related diseases, isn't it?" said Fraser. I didn't quite believe I'd heard either of them say what they'd just said, and my disbelief must have looked like stupidity or inattention or some such to him, for he added, as if reminding me of the topic of discussion, "Cholera."

"Yes," I said, "yes. People in Cité Carton get their water elsewhere and lug it in, or buy it from water-sellers who lug it part of the way in. The closest functioning pumps are miles away. Some of that water may be contaminated at the source. People are out making tests now. We—"

"What do you suppose the problem is," said Fraser mildly, "old pipes?"

Bazile frowned. "If it is old pipes, then it's a matter for the public works ministry—"

I was beginning to feel desperate. "Our main effort," I said, "is aimed at locating and cutting the source of the contaminated water, but we've also got sick people who need treatment. We need tetracycline if we can get it, streptomycin or chloramphenicol—"

"Have you asked the Albert Schweitzer Hospital," Britton said, "and the Baptist mission?"

"They have nothing to spare. Nobody has anything to spare."

She put on a thoughtful expression. "I suppose this must make you long to have the World Health Organisation back."

I bit off a reply to the effect that it sure hadn't been me who'd brought bankruptcy on the WHO. With the monied nations not paying their club dues, the United Nations had become a meeting hall for impoverished handwringers. The U.S. was spending every cent on things that either went boom or else went to Mars. The world's economic giants, such as they were, were so tight they squeaked. Countries like Haiti, Grenada, Burundi, and Nepal couldn't take up the slack.

I looked directly at her and said, "I'd settle for a planeload of antibiotics and I-V packs."

"I'm sorry," said Fraser, "I'm not sure what you think we can do."

"Haiti doesn't have the resources, but the United States still does."

"I see." His expression couldn't have been blander. "Is it bad?"

"Mister Fraser," I said, "I don't know what you think cholera is, but I'm here to tell you, it's virulent, nasty, and about as disgusting a disease as it's possible for humans to die of. God only knows how many infected people there are in Port-au-Prince right now, but every one of them's got a gutful of cholera bacteria. The bacteria produce toxins that disrupt the normal exchange of water and salts between the intestine and body tissues. Unabsorbed water and salts are eliminated in a profuse, continuous, watery diarrhea."

Britton crinkled her nose in disgust and said, "*Please*," and her soulmate looked annoyed and said, "Really, now." Bazile just looked interested.

I kept talking. "Cholera kills by dehydration. You want to drink a lot of water, but drinking water doesn't help. It just prolongs the diarrhea. Only intravenous replacement of fluids does the trick. And that's only part of the trick. The bacteria pass out of the body in stools, contaminate water and food, somebody comes along and ingests—"

"Stop it!" Fraser snapped, seizing my arm. We glared at each other for a second, and then I jerked away. He straightened his cuff, smiled icily, said, "There's nothing to be done for it. I've already discussed the matter with my government, but—" He shrugged.

Bazile looked put out. "It is too bad."

"Surely," I said, "if you explained the situation to them—"

"I'm sorry," said Fraser.

"There're two *million* people here!"

"It wouldn't matter if there were *ten* million. Now it's cholera. Last time, it was, ah—"

"Hepatitis."

"And *next* time, what will it be next time?" His expression was pitying. "Someone should explain the situation to *you*. Haiti's a filthy rathole, it's *been* a filthy rathole ever since these niggers threw the French out." Bazile didn't react to that; he was still too put out with Washington to mind a mere racial slur. "When you throw money down a rathole you throw it away, it's gone forever. Nobody has money to throw away these days. Even if they did, you think they'd give a damn about Haiti? *Haitians* don't even give a damn any more. You can hardly find a government in this place any more, because there's nothing to govern!"

"You're telling me," I said, "the United States can get men from the Earth to Mars but can't get a planeload of medical supplies from Santo Domingo to Port-au-Prince?"

He gestured toward the television screen, which was filled with images of space-suited individuals moving jerkily across a rock-littered landscape. "There," he said, "is the future. That's our next home."

"When do the folks from Cité Carton get to move in?"

He regarded me sourly. "If you look down all the time you never see the stars."

"While you're busy looking up," I said, "you may be sinking in your own crap."

"My advice to you is, take a vacation. No one should *want* to be here. I know *I* don't," and with that he gave Britton a look, and the two of them turned neatly and glided away, possibly to go make love on a bed of ice cubes, then lie around sucking marrow from the thigh bones of parboiled infants. The interview was concluded.

Bazile was philosophical as we rode back to Independence Square.

"Perhaps next time, he said, "everybody will get what he wants."

"Haiti can't get the time of day. You heard what he said. There's not going to be a next time."

"*Dèyè morne ginyin morne,*" he intoned.

"I know that proverb. Beyond every mountain, more mountains."

"You are not a Haitian," he said. "You do not read enough into it. It means not only that hardship follows hardship, but also that there is always hope. And next time, you and I will still be here, and that man back there will be back in America—"

"And someone just like him will have taken his place. Beyond every asshole, more assholes."

Bazile laughed. "Remember what I said about learning to do business with people you dislike. I can tell that you dislike me. Yet if I told you I know a few ways *around* the American government to these precious medical supplies—"

"Can we do business, monsieur, you and I?"

He looked good-naturedly doubtful. "I did say that these are *precious* medical supplies."

I said, "I have some money waiting for me at the American embassy."

"Oh?"

"How much tetracycline could I get for the price of a plane ticket to the States?"

He laughed again. "I love American humor," he said.

It was early evening when I stepped out of Bazile's car at Independence Square and sundown when I got back to the hospital. Dr de Rossarieu accepted the news of my second failure of the day with a sort of dreamy calm. I figured his unfocused equanimity put him half ahead of me; I was focused but upset. He told me to go change, wake Velmont, get back as soon as possible. Two more bluish, vomiting, helplessly shitting people had been brought in from Cité Carton, and the word was that still other people *weren't* being brought in. The *loas* were sending another punishment. We'd just have to do the best we could. An emergency meeting with people from the Albert Schweitzer Hospital and the Baptist mission was scheduled for nine pm. Someone claimed to have access to the last functioning police precinct in Port-au-Prince. De Rossarieu opined that the next time I went into Cité Carton, I'd have backup. The thought chilled me. It sounded like a sure-fire way to touch off a turf war between men with machetes and men wearing dark sunglasses. It did seem that bogeymen were all the government the country had at the moment.

I staggered out back to my room. Velmont was already awake. He sat on the edge of his bed and watched me work my shoes off my poor burning feet. There was American music on the radio. The signal from Miami was as strong and steady as it had been that morning, but the volume was turned down, and we could hear our stomachs growl at each other across the room.

"We need to eat," he said.

"A day like today," I said, "eating's just about the last thing I want to do."

"I didn't say anything about *wanting* to eat. I said, we *need* to eat."

"Not hungry. Anyway, there isn't time. The doc's still on his feet in the ward."

He started looking around for his socks. I hung up my good clothes, put on my not-so-good clothes, started to put on my shoes. I said to him, "Got anything to drink?"

"Maybe."

My eyes were stinging. I wouldn't let myself cry, wouldn't, but a sob escaped, I couldn't stop it, it just escaped.

"Velmont," I gasped "I feel, I feel like we're all here at the bottom of a mountain, trying to wave off an avalanche."

"I know the feeling."

The American music stopped, and the voice from the radio said that we would now hear highlights of the speech the president had made that morning. I switched off the radio in a fury.

"I don't want to hear another word about it," I said. "I don't want to hear another goddamn word about what a great moment it is. I don't want to hear how long it took to get men to Mars, and I *especially* goddamn don't want to hear how much it cost." I was panting, clutching one shoe, still fighting tears. "Know why I can't just give up here and go back to the States?"

Velmont shrugged and grinned. "You're a fugitive from American justice?" He was taking me seriously, in his own way. He was a good sort. He'd been doing all right in Montreal, where there was a Haitian community of about seventy thousand people. Then one day he'd found himself thinking long and hard about there being more Haitian physicians and nurses in Montreal than there were in all of Haiti. The next thing he knew, he was on a plane flying south.

"I imagine," I said, "I imagine what a shock it'd be to step on the plane *here*, step off *there*. Probably be even more of a shock than when I stepped off here. I imagine I get back to the States. Parts of it are still good places, the people are sleek and live so well. I imagine I'm walking around, marveling at how wonderful everything is. Then I hear somebody complain, it's just the least little thing, nothing good on TV tonight, beer's not cold enough, I don't know, but there's this *sound* in the back of my head like piano wire snapping, and I just start killing everybody, family, friends, total strangers. Everybody."

Neither of us spoke for several seconds.

Then he said, "It's not everybody's fault."

"It's *somebody's* fault."

"Well, killing everybody in the United States wouldn't fix Haiti. Won't even fix the United States. They have slums there, too."

"Not like here. Not like the City of Cartons."

Velmont gave me a look of friendly exasperation. "A slum's a slum. And, *tout' homme ce l'homme*. Every man is Man. Every woman, too. The U.S.'s bigger than Haiti. It's just taking them longer to run out of everything and start living in cartons."

We looked at each other for a long moment. Finally, I said, "You mentioned something about a drink."

"No, you did, but what the hey."

He opened his trunk and pulled out a bottle of Haitian rum, *clairin*, stuff so raw it could bring your dead ancestors back to life. He poured two glasses, gave one to me. We saluted each other, and I was about to take a sip when I saw him hesitate.

"A toast?" I said.

He raised his glass. "Fuck men on Mars," he said.

Our glasses touched.

Michael Bates Michael Bates Michael Bates Michael

Michael Bates himself, as he thought of himself, was swept away in a flood of Michael Bateses. He would have preferred to remain with the time machine, for he knew that he and it were central to whatever was happening here, but by the time he had got somewhat over the shock of seeing himself replicated, there were at least forty of him in the room, all shoving and jostling, and more arriving every second. He felt panic and knew he had to do something to keep from succumbing to it, so he called out, "Just stay where you are, everybody! Keep calm, and don't leave the room, and we'll figure out what the problem is."

But Michael Bateses quickly filled the room and spilled into adjoining rooms and corridors. Movement toward exits was immediate, almost instinctual.

"Okay, okay," said Michael Bates, trying to make himself heard above a growing din of voices as he was carried irresistibly forward, "let's just stop crowding and get ourselves straightened out and keep calm. Don't leave the building! *Don't* leave the building!"

"Keep calm yourself," another Michael Bates told him, "and stop blocking the corridor!"

"Yeah," said still another Michael Bates, "who do you think you are?"

"I *think*," said Michael Bates heatedly, "I'm the primary, essential, actual Michael Bates here!"

"Of course you do," said Michael Bates. "Each and every one of us must feel the way you do. Hurry along there."

"And each of us," said Michael Bates, "is sure he was the first to emerge from the machine, and all the rest of us are, ah, imitations. Better hurry along."

"As far as I know," said Michael Bates, "*I* was the first one out of the machine. But we're all so mixed up now, I don't know how to go about proving it. Hey, hurry along, before you get yourself trampled."

They struck the exit doors, flung them open with a resounding crash, emerged blinking into sunlight. Dozens and scores and hundreds of Michael Bateses hemorrhaged from the building into the parking lot. Here and there along the edge of the horde, they yelled such things as "Move it, move it!" and "Make way, make way!" at people who—this was just beginning to seem surprising—were not Michael Bates. Michael Bates himself, if it was he, shouted for everyone to keep calm, keep calm, and not leave the parking lot. There was a squeal of tires, and a car sped toward the main exit of the research complex. A great cry of anguish went after it from Michael Bateses who had been milling among the parked automobiles near the center of the lot, and a devastated Michael Bates suddenly turned and ran through the crowd screaming, "Somebody stole my car! Somebody just *drove off* in my car!"

"Were the keys in it?"

"He had his *own* keys! We've all got our *own* keys!"

The sounds of loss and fury worked their way outward from the center of the crowd to its edges, diminishing only as the news reached the door of the building where the time machine was housed. Michael Bateses continued to stream out, and each greeted word of the theft with the same thin cry of unhappiness. The stolen car had been dear to Michael Bates.

"I just don't understand what could've happened," said Michael Bates.

"Sloppiness happened," Michael Bates told him, or himself, as the case may have been. "When you set the automatic controls on the time machine, you carelessly arranged to have yourself return one second before you left."

"Are you saying—?"

"You're saying—"

"I'm—"

"We're—"

"Time-looped?"

They mulled it over for a moment.

Then Michael Bates flushed angrily and said, "Wait just a second, *I'm* the first Michael Bates, and I *checked* the setting on that timer before I left. I'm sure of it!"

"So am I!" said Michael Bates.

"Me, too!" said Michael Bates.

"Well, you messed up somehow."

"That setting was okay!"

"Obviously it wasn't!"

"Look, if you think I'm going to take the blame for this mess, you've got another—"

"Somebody's responsible for it!"

"*I'm* not!"

"*Some*body is."

"Not me!"

"Me neither!"

"Hey, don't look at me!"

"I *thought* I was looking at *him.*"

"Who?"

"How long can this go on?" Michael Bates asked no one in particular.

Some Michael Bates or other answered, "Until somebody thinks to shut off the time machine," and jerked his thumb over his shoulder in the direction of the laboratory building, "back *there.*"

Now far across the parking lot, the building sat like a forlorn island in a troubled sea of Michael Bateses.

Michael Bates shook his head and said, "Nobody's going to be able to go back against that tide!"

"Well," said Michael Bates, in a hopeful tone of voice, "maybe one of the Michael Bateses back there will think to turn off the machine before he gets pushed out of the laboratory."

"*We* didn't think of it," said Michael Bates, "until we were across the parking lot."

"Well," said the hopeful Michael Bates; or possibly the one standing next to him, "it doesn't mean that one of us *won't* instantly grasp what the situation is and turn off the machine."

"Doesn't mean one of us will, *either*," said a glum Michael Bates.

"If we're really all the same person here," Michael Bates said, "why aren't we thinking and saying and doing exactly the same thing here?"

"My name is legion," said the glum Michael Bates, very glumly. "I contain multitudes."

"Somebody'll figure out what to do," said Michael Bates, "sooner or later."

"I like *that*," said Michael Bates furiously, "sooner or later! It's been about twenty minutes since this thing started. At the rate we're coming out of the machine, about one per second, there're already about twelve hundred of us."

"Twelve hundred of *you*, you mean," said Michael Bates. "I still think I'm the one true Michael Bates."

"Aw, go chase yourself," said Michael Bates.

For the first time since things had gone awry, Michael Bates laughed. Some of him or them laughed, anyway.

"Well," said the Michael Bates who was the object of the laughter, "I *still* think I'm Michael Bates."

"But, seriously," said Michael Bates, "it comes out to thirty-six hundred of us an hour and more than eighty-six *thousand* of us per day!"

"It'll never go that far!" said Michael Bates.

"No?" Michael Bates looked around at his faces. "Who'll stop it? The board of trustees? The police? The military? A panel of experts? Public opinion? Act of Congress?"

"Well," said Michael Bates, "*somebody*'ll stop it."

"How *soon*?" said Michael Bates.

Michael Bates was silent for a moment. Then he looked around and saw that the parking lot was almost full of Michael Bateses and said, "Time to move across the street, I think," and he and his immediate group of duplicates began to move, not only across the street but toward the exits as well. They could hear sirens approaching, and a helicopter. At the edge of the crowd, Michael Bates exhorted everyone to keep calm and remain in the complex.

"Don't any of you dare call Missis Bates," he was saying, "and don't all have to go to the men's room at once, and *don't use the credit cards!*"

Meanwhile, Michael Bateses continued to come out of the time machine in the room in the building with the parking lot in the research complex on the block in the city in the county of the state of the nation on the continent in the hemisphere of the planet.

Look Away

At sunset the bluffs below Memphis burned. Tangled, leafless trees along the Arkansas bank seemed to writhe against a backdrop of flame-reddened sky. Until then the war had been far away and as long ago as last year's bad dreams, but suddenly I was put irresistibly in mind of burning towns and ruined countrysides.

At my side, Colonel Soileau puffed on his cigar and looked content. "It's mighty good," he said, "to be on this old river again. None of those tricklets back East quite compares."

"They say the Amazon puts even the Mississippi to shame."

"Then it truly must be something to take a look at. We'll just have to go see for ourselves, won't we?"

I made no reply, and after a moment my subdued mood must have registered on him, for he said, "Having second thoughts?"

"Some small, scattered ones, sir, I have to confess. There was a straightforwardness in being a cavalryman that is missing from this enterprise. And I find that I'm more afraid of failure now than I have ever been before."

The colonel removed the cigar from his mouth and turned his head to look at me. His face was weirdly highlighted in the commingled glow of setting sun and kerosene lantern. With his glittering eyes and his bushy white eyebrows that met above the bridge of a great hooked beak of a nose, he had the look of a night-hunting bird. I had known battle-weary soldiers to express a preference for having Minié balls whiz about their persons rather than be transfixed with the old man's awful glare.

Yet his manner with me was kindly. "Heaven knows," he murmured, "that perils attend our enterprise." He spoke so softly that I barely heard him above the sound of the paddle wheel, He made a gesture that took in Mississippi to the east, Arkansas to the west, and everything beyond each. "This could be the breaking and not the making of us all. So, entertain as many doubts as you like until our rendezvous with the cruiser. I hope that I may still be able to rely upon you then."

"Colonel—"

"I have always been able to rely upon you. Shall we go into the saloon now? The sight and sound of all this water have made me powerfully thirsty."

"Of course, sir."

In the saloon I saw Mayhew, the cotton merchant. We had met him first thing upon boarding at Memphis, and I had quickly found him to be an obsequious bore. Now he was sitting at a table with two other men. He indicated with a wave that we were welcome to join his party, and I could only repress a groan as Colonel Soileau headed straight for him. There were not many other people in the saloon, and none that we knew, and we were therefore trapped by etiquette. In one corner a handful of musicians plucked at and tootled over "Dixie."

Mayhew and his companions stood to receive us. The older of these, whose empty right sleeve was pinned neatly to the breast of his frock coat, was introduced to us as Major Pennell, "late of the Army of Northern Virginia." The younger man was Bradley Mayhew. It took me a moment to see any resemblance between the cotton merchant and his son: Mayhew *pere* was blocky and coarse-faced; Mayhew *fils* was fine-featured and fair—probably about nineteen years old. His handshake was clammy, and he could barely meet the colonel's fierce eye, but he gave me what I interpreted as some kind of hopeful look. I was closest to him in age, having only part of a decade on him. I was introduced simply as "Gravois, Colonel Soileau's secretary." As the five of us sat down, a steward brought extra glasses and more whiskey.

"Would you be the Colonel Soileau," Major Pennell said, "who served on Albert Johnston's staff during the campaigns in Tennessee and Ohio?"

"I am the one, sir. I was with Beauregard at Charleston, too."

"The colonel was there when the shooting started," I put in, just like a good little toady, "and there when it stopped." This appeared to go well with the Mayhews, but Major Pennell merely gave a soft grunt to acknowledge that he had heard me. He was sharper than he looked, I decided, and I had better be careful of him.

To Colonel Soileau, he said, "Even in Virginia we heard how one of Johnston's staff officers, a man somewhat advanced in years, rallied a regiment at Shiloh, after all of its officers had been killed or wounded, and hit the Yankee line like Hell itself." Major Pennell grinned around his cigar at young Mayhew. "That's how the journalists described it, Mr Mayhew: 'Like Hell itself.'"

The youth regarded Colonel Soileau very intently and said, stammeringly, "Then I salute you, sir, and—I envy you!"

An instant after he had delivered himself of that, he crimsoned to the roots of his macassared hair. His father struggled to conceal his own embarrassment. Suddenly I understood: young Mayhew had sat out the war in his father's trading office somewhere, and hated himself for it, and perhaps hated his father as well far letting him do it. It is a soldier's inalienable right to despise all civilians as slackers, and yet I found that my contempt for the young man was outweighed by an unexpected and morbid curiosity about him. Perhaps his father had even encouraged him to do it, and now sought to make some kind of amends by forcing the company of soldiers and ex-soldiers on him. Or, alternatively, perhaps the father had not been so encouraging, and intended the company of soldiers as torture.

As I entertained these and other unpleasant speculations, Major Pennell touched his empty sleeve and said to the colonel, "Young Mayhew does not envy me entirely, of course. In my case, the Yankees happened to hit back like Hell itself."

His voiced lacked any trace of bitterness, and yet his words must have smashed to bits whatever self-esteem Bradley Mayhew still possessed. They even had a sobering effect on the senior Mayhew for several seconds. Then that lumpish individual brightened and began to burble.

"Nevertheless," he said, diplomatically swivelling his gaze back and forth between the two officers, "you two saw history being made. You helped to make it, in fact." He remembered me, finally. "Oh, and you must have been one of our brave heroes in gray, too, Mr. Gravois."

"I was a cavalry courier, Mr. Mayhew, and I wore butternut. I saw a great deal of hard riding, but hardly any fighting." I could have added that I had seen the Ohio Valley scorched virtually from end to end.

Colonel Soileau gently chided me. "Do not be so dismissive of yourself, Gravois. You performed an invaluable service. You will be able to say to your children and grandchildren, 'I carried dispatches!'"

"Yes," Major Pennell added, "it has more of a swing to it than, 'I lost an arm to a Yankee bullet.'"

The remark was in very poor taste, and for a moment, Colonel Soileau seemed about to employ his formidable frown. He thought better of it, however, and made a gallant essay with, "Major, I fear our time may soon be past. Ours is a young nation, and it is young men like Gravois here, and young Mayhew"—Bradley Mayhew flinched as the colonel's owl gaze settled upon him for a second— "who will be making its history from now on."

Old Mayhew said, "Gentleman, let us now raise our glasses in a toast."

We raised our glasses.

"To the Confederate States of America," the cotton merchant intoned. "Long may they prosper!"

We solemnly echoed the sentiment and drained our glasses. I noticed that, young as he was, Bradley Mayhew knew how to inhale whiskey. His father immediately refilled everyone's glass, then gave Major Pennell an expectant look.

The major rose to the occasion. "To all who fought for the South, couriers as well as colonels. May God bless every man who defied oppression and helped to secure the defeat of the tyrant Lincoln!"

"Hear, hear!" And we drained our glasses a second time.

It was my turn next. I got by with a paraphrase of a toast I had once heard Albert Sidney Johnston raise to the ladies of the Confederacy.

Major Pennell smacked his lips softly and looked at me. "The colonel is right. Now that the fighting and marching are all over, we're all supposed to go home and get on with our lives. I imagine that things are going to seem awfully dull for some of us from now on. But what do the Confederacy's young men propose to do with themselves?"

I gave him a tight-feeling smile. "Some are headed to New Orleans, thence to Galveston, to seek their fortunes in Texas."

"Well, Texas could he exciting, I imagine," said old Mayhew, too heartily.

"I understand there are still Indians to fight in Texas," said young Mayhew, too earnestly. I was past even morbid curiosity by this time; the Mayhews had begun to make my skin crawl.

"The army," Major Pennell said, too drily, "has pushed the Indians rather farther west than Galveston."

"The army has no business fighting Indians in Texas!" The colonel spoke the word *Indians* as though it tasted bad, "Let those so-called Rangers fight Indians. Soldiers need a real enemy."

The Mayhews looked taken aback by this outburst. The major nodded and said—again, too drily—"Yes, we *have* got to keep our pride."

For my part, I could already feel the warmth from the whiskey, and I was watching the colonel closely. Anyone who did not know him probably would have thought that he was taking his liquor very well, but I knew him and knew that a little whiskey went a long way with him. If his outburst were not enough, I could have told by the reddening of his eye and the thickening of his speech that he had already veered toward the rim of the abyss.

Then, to my further dismay, old Mayhew, having made certain that the glasses were full again, turned to the colonel and said, "I believe it is now your turn to propose the toast."

Without a moment's hesitation, Colonel Soileau raised his glass and said, "To Mexico, Cuba, and Brazil," and if I had not been stunned by his recklessness, I would have wished that lightning had blasted him on the spot before he uttered the second syllable. As if by afterthought, and as though he had not said enough already, he added, "And to wars to come!"

The Mayhews gave each other astonished looks. Major Pennell started, but recovered instantly and, with his glass still raised, said, as mildly as though he were giving someone the time of day, "The Confederacy has already fought the only war it needs to fight, sir. Fought and won it."

The colonel puckered his hairy brow and replied, "Major, it is our manifest destiny. Just as the United States must push westward, we must push southward."

"But to speak of foreign adventures now, when our nation is still practically impoverished—" Major Pennell half-turned to old Mayhew. "Is your business now nearly as good as it was in 1860?"

"Well," the cotton merchant began, but Colonel Soileau cut him short with a growl.

"All the more reason," he said, "to move quickly—before the army is completely dismantled. The Southern fighting man is one of our great assets. He is the equal of any soldier in the world, even of the French—I say that as a proud descendant of the warrior race of Europe. Moreover, no navy in the world is a match for our ironclads. And the *Alabama* is the finest cruiser afloat!"

"Certainly Southern fighting men performed prodigies on the battlefield, Colonel, but they had the best reasons men ever have. I will go so far as to say that they had the only just reasons—they were defending their homes and fighting for their liberty. But Mexico and Cuba are different propositions. I doubt if one butternut in ten even knows where Brazil is, let alone how he might get there or what business he might have there."

The two officers had gradually lowered their glasses to the table during this exchange, and the rest of us had quietly followed suit. The toast was forgotten. Color was creeping into the colonel's normally sallow cheek, and a scowl had taken up permanent residence on the major's face. Some men of my acquaintance probably would have left off arguing at about this point and challenged, and others would have brandished their canes, but the colonel's age and the major's empty sleeve ruled out such options. The officers were locked in this argument till death, or least through an evening, unless someone intervened. I pressed my foot hard against the colonel's under the table, but he would not look my way. I tried by effort of will alone to get him to shut up. I might as well have tried to will a cyclone into submission.

"Just put a good man like Johnston or your Robert Lee or Tom Jackson at the head of a Confederate Army," the colonel was saying, rapping the tabletop for emphasis, "and you will see how easily Southern fighting men can find their way anywhere in the Western Hemisphere."

"That sounds familiar," the major responded, in a tone of voice that stopped just short of sarcasm. "I recall a time, not long ago, when my comrades and I had every expectation of marching straight from Richmond to Washington within a week's time. We thought that Yankees wouldn't give us much of a fight. We learned differently at Manassas and Sharpsburg."

"I'll see your Manassas and Sharpsburg, Major, and raise you Shiloh and Cincinnati. And I'll tell you this, sir—there isn't another army in the Americas that could give us the sort of fight we had at Shiloh. That was a stand-up fight between white men. I was with Scott in Mexico in the forties. We defeated one armed mob of overdressed greasers after another. We lost fewer men in the whole campaign than were killed on picket duty on a typical day in Ohio. The only thing standing between us and the Strait of Magellan now is a lot of greasers and niggers." He shot a quick look at Bradley Mayhew. "And *Indians*."

While young Mayhew had tried to make himself unobtrusive, and I fumed helplessly, old Mayhew had watched in obvious horror as the argument ran away with his table guests. His expression was that of a man whose expectations had been most cruelly thwarted. Now, however, at last he had seen what evidently appeared to him as an opportunity to deflect the officers' mounting antipathy from each other and toward a third party. Sweaty, red-faced, he put on what was intended as a smile but looked like a grimace, and said, "This fellow Juárez who's *president* of Mexico now, I believe he is an Indian. How can Texas stand to have such a country for a neighbor?"

Major Pennell looked at him as though he had just descended from the moon, but the cotton merchant's remark had the effect of pouring kerosene on Colonel Soileau's fire. The colonel slammed his fist down on the tabletop with enough force to cause amber liquid to slop over the rims of the forgotten glasses, and he said "*Exactly!*" with such extraordinary vehemence that conversation momentarily ceased throughout the saloon. I saw faces turn toward us. Even the musicians faltered at their slaughter of "Marching Through Maryland."

I made a show of consulting my watch and said, "Colonel, we really must hurry if we are to have our supper."

"Hang supper, Gravois." Though he spoke to me, he did not take his eyes off Major Pennell, who met his gaze levelly. "Major, any single well-publicized incident—an exchange of gunfire along the Rio Grande, let us say—would suffice. Texans don't like greasers as a matter of course, and the other Confederate States would back Texas, just as all backed South Carolina after Fort Sumter. There is another, best, just reason for soldiers of the South to fight—to establish and maintain the white race's primacy. And think of what else we would gain. Not just territory and treasure, but a true bonding of our people, a cementing together of the Confederacy!"

The major managed to shake his head without breaking eye contact. "Perhaps the states don't want to be permanently cemented together. I understand that, at the height of the war, Georgia considered seceding from the secession."

"That was a seditious rumor, spread by Yankee spies! The Confederacy can survive only if the states stand by one another."

"The baboon Lincoln said essentially as much in defense of the Union," Major Pennell drawled, "and we disputed at length with him."

Colonel Soileau opened his mouth to deliver some retort of his own, but I placed my hand upon his arm and interjected, "Sir, we really must be going now." I had had quite enough. His cheeks were already aglow; now his whole face began to mottle. He turned toward me and regarded my offending grasp as though deciding which of my fingers to bite off. Ordinarily, I would have quailed before his glare, removed my hand, and apologized. There was too much at stake, however. If I had come somewhat later than he to wholehearted belief in the rightness of what we were about—for God, country, and President Davis—then I was prepared to go as far with him as I must. Better that I should take liberties with him now and risk one evening of his wrath than let him imperil our mission.

He looked from my hand to my face and must have read therein my determination, for he set his mouth against whatever harsh words he had been about to loose, and nodded, first to me, then to the others.

"You must forgive me, gentlemen," he said, "especially you, Major Pennell. Ours is a new nation. It is only too easy for one to be carried away by one's own enthusiasm."

Major Pennell accepted that with a gracious little speech of his own, to the effect that enthusiasm, after all, had carried them as far as Cincinnati and the Yankee Capital itself. He ruined it, however, by saying at the end, "There is nothing like being fetched up short by a Minié ball, Colonel, to dampen a man's enthusiasm."

The colonel gave him a smile as thin as the edge of a razor, nodded once more to the Mayhews, and strode out of the saloon with me close on his heels. He moved straight to the rail and gripped it with such force that I half-expected the wood to crack in his grasp. He said nothing for a time, but stared out across the water towards Arkansas.

Finally he looked along his shoulder at me. "Gravois, that man is the next-worse thing after a traitor."

I said, rather sharply, "Forget him, Colonel. He is a bitter man trying to amuse himself."

"His kind would have us stand pat, have us *sit!* We are bound for empire, and he would have us be a quiet, inconsequential little nation of—of planters and plowmen!"

"You shouldn't have let him annoy you, sir. And if we are to succeed, it is not just you who must rely upon me. I must rely upon you. No more proselytizing to strangers! We are just two peaceful citizens, a retired army officer and his secretary, on a business trip to New Orleans."

"How can we succeed, Gravois, with men like Pennell—and half-men like that Mayhew? Ugh!"

"They aren't typical. At least, let us hope that young Mayhew isn't. Perhaps he'll even be grateful for a second chance to do his duty. And even a man as cynical as Major Pennell may come around, once men like you have set things in motion.'

We would be in Cuba before the month was out, and so, too, the *Alabama*, paying a friendly visit. By this time next month, if all went reasonably according to plan, the cruiser would be at the bottom of Havana Harbor, the Confederacy would resound with cries of "Remember the *Alabama!*" and we would have our war with Spain. And by this time next year, who could say? Who can see the end of anything? Mexico, perhaps, or Haiti. There were Caribbean islands that were ours for the taking, if we could but get to New Orleans without Colonel Soileau's telling everyone on the Mississippi what we were about.

"Now, come, sir," I said, "and let us get our supper."

He put out his hand for me to take, and murmured, "Yes, of course." I barely heard him above the sound of the paddle wheel as it turned ceaselessly, propelling us down the great river, into deepening darkness.

Edge of the Wind

The road wound through thick jungle. The driver chattered happily
about the island's natural splendors and seemed to know his
botany, for he would nod and point and say, "That is breadfruit,"
or "Poinsettia," or "Gommier." Anita, who felt barely competent
to distinguish grass from trees, would dutifully look, only to see the
same dark threatening wall of greenery.

"We grow everything good to eat," said the driver. "Banana,
orange, pimento. Cacoa for the chocolate. And smell that good
smell." She did detect traces of something pleasant in the car's
hot-motor-and-old-upholstery atmosphere. "Every spice you want
grows right here. Cinnamon, nutmeg, cloves, mace."

From time to time, they passed through clearings, and she saw
huts and dark-skinned people whose expressions communicated
nothing. One old man agitatedly shook a stick adorned with
feathers and bones. She stared until the car had rounded a bend in
the road, then asked MacLeish, seated beside her, "What was that
all about?"

"Island magic," he said mildly. "Some disgruntled islander just
tried to wish us away."

"Why?"

MacLeish's beard framed a grin. "Maybe he spotted us for
Americans. Maybe he just hates white people generally." He called
to the driver. "What do you think?"

The driver did not look around. "Could be, boss."

"The matter of race," MacLeish said, "goes back centuries. The matter of Americans goes back to the invasion. Not everyone here was happy to have Marines shooting up the place." He called to the driver again. "Isn't that so?"

"Could be, boss."

MacLeish laughed. He was sweaty and happy. Anita tried to relax, failed, contented herself with wishing that the driver would negotiate turns more cautiously. He appeared unfazed when the car missed annihilating a group of half naked children by inches. Come all this way, Anita thought, to get killed in a car wreck.

There had been no question of her not coming. MacLeish had simply invited her to join him aboard his *Martha Ann* in the West Indies. "We'll start at the bottom," he had told her, "at St. George's, on the south side of Grenada. We'll sail all the way up to the Virgins." She had simply accepted. There was no way in the world she was going to turn down an offer of a Caribbean cruise. A Caribbean cruise, like caviar or an expensive car or a diamond bracelet, was just one of those things she knew she desired before she knew whether or not she liked them. MacLeish was another; there was no way she was going to let him go anywhere without her if she could help it. The relationship had possibilities.

Thus she had passed from Dallas-Fort Worth International to an island airfield that looked a block long and a yard wide. That was at Grenville, at the far end of Grenada from the port of St. George's. Now she was crammed with MacLeish and too much luggage into a taxi making its rattling, un-air-conditioned way along the island's undulating spine.

The car crested a final ridge. Before them, the road twisted past cultivated plots, and Anita found herself looking down an uneven slope at rooftops, streets, the harbor of St. George's itself. The harbor was the inundated crater of an extinct volcano but looked the size of a teacup. Past its mouth, the calm, glittering Caribbean stretched away to the horizon.

"There's *Martha Ann* down there," MacLeish said.

Anita peered. Craft of all descriptions cluttered the harbor. "I have no idea what to look for."

"Thirty-eight footer."

"You're talking to someone who doesn't know a canoe from an aircraft carrier." She pretended to peer again. "Mac, nobody's eyes are that good."

"Trust me."

"I trust you, I just don't think I believe you."

The driver called back over his shoulder, "You want to go on down to your boat, boss?"

"No, no, the hotel."

The hotel directly overlooked the harbor. By the time Anita and MacLeish had cleaned themselves up and changed clothes, it was almost sundown. Burgett sent word that he was waiting in the bar. It was cool there, and crowded with casually well-dressed white people. Burgett was drinking alone at a table, a wiry ageless man with sun-bleached hair and a complexion like a brick's. He greeted MacLeish easily but hesitated before shaking the hand Anita offered. His palm was hard as the bottom of a patent-leather shoe. As they sat down, he said, "Pleasant flight?" and MacLeish shrugged and replied, "Absolutely uneventful. The car ride from Grenville's more interesting."

"Always is."

Anita said, "An old man shook a stick at us."

"What?" Burgett looked at her blankly.

"He shook a stick at us."

Burgett said, "Ah," plainly not understanding, then, to MacLeish—tuning out Anita as casually as though he were changing television channels—"Roger's finished stocking the boat. But he won't be going this time. Says the signs are bad."

"Signs?" MacLeish looked surprised. "Weather?"

"Hell, no. Now who are you going to trust, the weather service or a rummy old bugger? It's just some bloody island nonsense."

"This is short notice."

"Only takes me to handle the yawl rig."

"Still. It won't be quite the same without Roger." To Anita, who had, sat quietly annoyed during this exchange, MacLeish said, "Roger's a local character. He's been with me on all my other cruises."

Burgett took a drink and wiped his mouth with the back of his hand.

His gaze flicked away from MacLeish, did not quite alight on Anita, flicked back to MacLeish. "Be crowded as it is."

"I take up hardly any room at all," Anita said, batting her eyelashes, "and, anyway, I know how to keep out from under men's big feet. I'll stay down in the kitchen while you sail Mac's boat for him. I'll knit some nice doilies for all the deck chairs."

Burgett looked at her in surprise, looked to MacLeish for some kind of support which he evidently did not quite receive, looked down at his I drink in confusion.

"Galley," said MacLeish, grinning. "It's not a kitchen, it's a galley. And there're no deck chairs." He trained the grin specifically on Burgett. "I should warn you about her. Sassy thing. Hardly defers to me at all. She needs a warning label. A t-shirt printed with the words, *Not MacLeish's Usual Sort of Bimbo*."

Anita said, "That's supposed to be a compliment," and smiled her third-best smile, a thin one. She hated the word *bimbo*.

There was an eruption of laughter from a nearby table. MacLeish and Burgett ignored it but Anita looked toward the source, two almost identical young white men sitting with two almost identical women of darker complexion. She had never seen any of the four before, but she knew the men—the boys, as she immediately thought of them—to be first-time visitors from the States as certainly as though they had sat across the aisle from her on the plane in. They drank, in a manner of speaking, with both hands. The two women, whom they appeared to be determined to impress, sipped their drinks, or pretended to, smiled whenever their escorts happened to look their way, and took no part in the conversation. The boys—she christened them Ned and Ted—were playing a diagnostic version of Jeopardy.

"An infectious contagious tropical disease," Ned would say, "caused by a spirochete," and rattle his ice, "characterized by ulcerating lesions and bone involvement."

"What is yaws?" Ted would say, looking smug, Both would pause to take a drink. Then Ted would say: "Okay, my turn. Ah. An iron-deficiency anemia in young girls, characterized by a greenish color of the skin."

"Gimme a break—what is chlorosis?" Pause, gulp. "Um. A painful swelling of the leg at childbirth, caused by inflammation and clotting in the veins."

"What is milk leg?" Pause. Gulp.

Anita wondered whether the boys were actually doctors at all. They were awfully young and altogether too incompletely formed to be full-fledged medical practitioners. Perhaps they were only interns. Perhaps they were med students. But since when did either interns or med students have the time and the wherewithal to hang out in hotel bars on Caribbean islands? Perhaps they were burned-out interns, then, or washed-out med students. Well, she thought, whoever, whatever, they might be, they certainly didn't seem to realize that people weren't impressed with what doctors knew, but with how much money they made.

The harbor of St. George's lay in the deep shadow of the island itself when they went to board the boat. MacLeish had described *Martha Ann* as an ocean cruiser-racer, sturdy enough for the open seas and yet of shallow enough draft, thanks to a centerboard, to work close in to shore—none of which meant a thing to Anita. He claimed to have sailed it, sailed "her," in the local Easter regatta. All Anita knew was that it was required of her that she think *Martha Ann* beautiful, even in that gloom, even at that unreasonable hour, even amid an armada of trim sloops and schooners. Accordingly, she told MacLeish she thought the boat was beautiful. He had been gazing upon it with real and obvious tenderness, but at hearing the object of his regard complimented he put on an expression of fine manly pride of possession.

He took her aboard and below and showed her the sleeping quarters, the tiny galley, the tinier head. The bunk, she noted, was definitely made for two. MacLeish gave her a wink and said, "The mate likes to sleep up on deck." Both the stove and the table were gimbaled. The refrigerator was stocked with delicacies. MacLeish took out a bottle of champagne, poured two glasses, proposed a toast. Champagne breakfast on a yacht, Anita thought. Perfect. She sipped and looked around and said, "People've tried to rent me smaller efficiency apartments."

The sky was lightening, though the sun remained out of sight behind the island, when *Martha Ann* ghosted out of St. George's. The town came right down to the water, and even at that early hour busy people thronged the streets and crowded the shore. The boat passed under the antique guns of the fort guarding the mouth of the harbor and turned parallel with Grenada's black leeward flank. MacLeish helmed, Burgett tended sail, and Anita had nothing to do but stay out of the way and enjoy the smell and the feel of the sea, the taste of salt on her lips, and the rhythmic action of the sharp bow as it sliced the waves. After a time, the sun shyly peeked over the island's spine, and a pale and smoky world was revealed, of haze-softened peaks, jungle, and fishing communities barely big enough to qualify as villages. By contrast, *Martha Ann's* white hull and sails and polished wood and fittings were luminous. Anita spotted a small craft far out to sea. It looked as fragile as eggshell. Tiny human figures knelt in it; they could have been praying. She pointed and said concernedly, "Are they lost?"

MacLeish shook his head. "You wouldn't believe how far the local fishermen will go out in those little *gommiers* of theirs. You navigate by sight in the West Indies. They've been doing it for centuries. All you have to know is that the islands are somewhere off to your east, so all you have to do to get home is find an island, recognize it, and make your way accordingly."

"What if you don't recognize it?"

"Ha! Then you've got no business being on the water. Sail these islands a time or two, you get to know them at a glance. Hardly any of them is completely out of sight of another island, and no two are exactly alike. That's true whether you're seeing them from a boat or prowling around them on foot. This is the world's real melting pot. You've got your French, Dutch, Spanish, Africans, Caribs, Asians, and every combination thereof. You got your Martians, too. We're the people from Mars." He beckoned to her. "Come steer."

"What? You want me to—"

"Sure. Nothing to it."

He made a space between himself and the wheel, and she moved into it. He showed her where to place her hands, how not to let the boat get away from her. For a time, he rested his hands over hers, transmitting their strength and expertise through her. They were big heavy hands with hairy backs, not, she reflected, your usual investment genius's kind of hand. She suddenly realized that he had relaxed. He still had his arms about her, was still pressed closely and excitingly against her from behind, but she was guiding *Martha Ann*. An inexpressible elation filled her. She glimpsed Burgett forward. He spared her only a quick, unimpressed glance.

Later, when they were approaching Grenada's northern end, MacLeish murmured into her ear, "Better go buckle down for a rough ride," and took the wheel from her. "Oilskins in the locker." He gestured forward. "Going to be rough in the channel up ahead."

The wind abruptly seemed to rebound from Grenada as the island dropped astern. The boat lifted to big rollers, fell, buried itself to the stanchions, and spray came across the deck in sheets. MacLeish bawled to Burgett to reef, and Burgett scrambled to tend jib, mizzen, and mainsail. Even with reduced sail the boat seemed hard-pressed to accommodate so much wind. Anita clung to a stanchion. She could feel the vessel straining, and as a particularly powerful puff pushed it down like a great invisible hand she half expected it to fly apart at the joins. Water millraced over the cabin trunk and lee deck, then fell away abruptly; hanging from the stanchion, she stared down into a swirling black-green pit. She did not know whether to be exhilarated or merely frightened out of her wits until MacLeish shot her a glance over his shoulder. He was grinning his grin. She thought, My God, it's *Hemingway*, and decided on exhilaration. MacLeish bellowed his own joy at the sky. "Golf is for *pussies!*"

The wind finally faltered as they drew abreast of a tiny island, and *Martha Ann* righted itself. Anita let go of the stanchion. She had held on to it throughout the passage. Her fingers were numb, her wrist ached. "That," she said breathlessly, "was quite a ride."

"Hope you liked it," MacLeish said. "Plenty more like it ahead. The West Indies separate the Atlantic and the Caribbean. Winds and waves that started at Africa have to come through the gaps between the islands."

Burgett went below as soon as they had put the anchor down off Carriacou. After an interval, he announced dinner. It was delicious, and Anita said so. Burgett acknowledged the compliment with a nod and a murmur. Then he sat back with a drink in his hand while MacLeish held forth at length about the joys of flogging canvas compared with other hair-raising experiences. He spoke so entertainingly of even the arcana of sail and line that Anita waited until late that night to say, "I don't think Burgett likes me."

"What do you care, as long as I like you?"

They were lying on the oversized bunk in a loose tangle of bare limbs. Old, sweet music played softly, "I Surrender, Dear," "Moonglow," "Stardust". They had made love twice; it was, she reflected during the lull, like sitting on a volcano. Now she had her fingers thrust into the dense mat of MacLeish's chest hair and her face half buried in his beard. His smell of salt and whiskey was intoxicating.

"I just wonder," Anita said, "if I've done something to irritate him. Or does he think women on boats are bad luck?"

"Haven't you ever met a misogynist before?"

"Oh, all the time."

MacLeish shifted in the darkness and stroked her back. "He's a professional sailor, one of the best I've ever known. I think he's probably only truly happy when he's sailing."

"No wife and kids, no—no life ashore?"

"Sure. No wife and kids, but lots of gambling. He loves to gamble. Horse races, cockfights."

"Ugh. Grown men watching chickens kill one another."

"It's the local action. Probably keeps Burg from drinking himself to death or chasing bimbos." That word again. "My guess is he thinks that sailing, gambling, and women are about equally unpredictable propositions, and a man's asking for trouble if he tries to handle all three."

"How sad. He's shut out half the human race."

"It's his life. Besides." MacLeish grunted happily and pulled her to him. "More for me."

They worked their way northward through the Grenadines the following morning, alternately lazing gracefully along the leeward shores and plunging at full tilt across the channels. Their landfall was the Tobago Cays, in a lagoon sheltered behind a cluster of islets. Anita and MacLeish snorkeled on the reef and explored one of the uninhabited islets, a small, steep-sided spur of overgrown volcanic rock fringed with white sand. They climbed to its summit and admired the view. MacLeish planted his feet wide, put his fists on his hips, made an expansive sound. She believed she knew how he felt. She said, "We could be a million miles from the rest of the world." Somewhere over the horizon was Dallas, where she had a successful small publishing business and a comfortable home and money in the bank and good friends and a life. She realized with a little start that she had not once thought about them since leaving St. George's. "I almost wouldn't mind staying right here forever."

"Almost is the operative word. I come down here once a year, sail, fish, carry on—and experience a rare contentment. From a yacht, the islands are paradise. But for the locals, they're the Third World. And, sooner or later, usually sooner, I get restless. I start wondering how things are shaping up back in the real world. Back in my real life. Making money also fills me with contentment, you know." He reached for her. "Making love, too."

"Beast," she said, resisting only very feebly and briefly.

Their next stop was Kingstown, St. Vincent, where they spent two days shopping and sightseeing and two evenings dining, dancing, and drinking. The first night, they made love almost until dawn in a good hotel room overlooking the harbor. The second, they returned to *Martha Ann* early, and at five o'clock in the morning the boat slipped quietly out to sea again. Approaching the northern end of St. Vincent, MacLeish pointed out the hazy blue heights of the volcano Soufrière and told her that it had erupted in 1902 and killed fifteen hundred people. Then he waved airily with the sandwich she had made for him and added, "But that's nothing. Pelée, on Martinique, blew up the next day and killed thirty thousand." Burgett squatted forward; Anita had made a sandwich for him as well, and he ate it slowly, almost cautiously, while he studied the horizon. That evening, they put the anchor down at Castries, St. Lucia, but MacLeish said that they would not go ashore, Castries was a raw kind of town, he was too tired for it.

He was not too tired for sex, however. It left Anita feeling less as though she had been sitting on a volcano and more as though she had been riding a mechanical bull. She was quietly grateful when he finally dropped off to sleep. She pulled on her cut-offs and a flannel shirt and left the cabin. Burgett was on deck, smoking a cigarette. He went forward when she came up, and she glared at his retreating back. For God's sake, she thought, it was just a sandwich! She sat aft, admired the harbor lights, listened attentively when music floated out from shore. She felt cut off from everybody and everything and could not decide whether that made her sad or happy. Dallas seemed like a dream. There was everything to be said for being on a boat on a calm warm sea, right?

She had, of course, been filling out her MacLeish checklist all along. She resisted the urge to tally pluses and minuses. She was feeling the first stirrings of apprehension about the totals. MacLeish had looks and energy and money-making acumen, he made every other man she had ever known look like a wax dummy, and better a man who was on too much than one who was never on at all.

But he's too big a dynamo for this little boat, she thought, and gave the wood trim an affectionate slap. We should be on a cruise liner, or a battleship....

In Fort-de-France, Martinique, they dined on *escargots* and *caneton à l'orange* in a small bistro. Midway through the meal, MacLeish received a hand-delivered message from an old acquaintance. "We're invited to visit Monsieur Léopoldie at his country home," he said. "I handle business for him on the Third Coast. He's Caribbean planter aristocracy, a *béké*—a white descendant of French colonists."

A hired car took them inland, following a road that mounted into a dark, precipitous countryside. The Léopoldie house was huge. It sat upon a terrace of pale brick, itself set on a natural rise; Anita felt that she could have looked not only straight down into Fort-de-France but clear across the Caribbean as well, to Central America and beyond to the Pacific. A mulatto servant greeted them at the door and led them from the jalousied porch to a high-ceilinged room. There were shelves of books, silver cups, a crucifix mounted on the wall. The master of the house was a long, distinguishedly gray man in his sixties. He bounded up from his cane chair and shook MacLeish's hand warmly. "How good to see you again!" He had a rich accent. He peered at Anita as though he had first-refusal rights, and she gave him her second-best smile.

They moved to a verandah on another side of the house. A different mulatto served rum punch, and MacLeish and the planter bent their heads together and conversed about boats, horses, and money while Anita sat quietly and opened her mouth only to take a sip of her drink. Then MacLeish suddenly stopped talking and turned his face toward the open windows. Anita listened. There was a sound of drumming, faint, as if coming from a great distance, yet insistent. MacLeish, after listening or a moment, said, "The natives are restless tonight," and smiled at his own wit.

"They are restless most nights," said Monsieur Léopoldie. Anita looked questioningly at him. His mouth twisted in a grimace. "*Quimbois.*"

She shook her head uncomprehendingly and started to apologize for her imperfect French, but MacLeish snapped, "*Quimbois*—local black magic, right?"

Léopoldie nodded.

"Only the label changes," MacLeish said.

Léopoldie said it again, "*Quimbois,*" made a but-of-course gesture, went on, "*obeah, vodou,* yes, only the label."

"Go anywhere in the Caribbean," MacLeish told Anita, "even Cuba, and you find essentially the same pack of soothsayers and spellcasters praying to the same pack of transplanted African gods and *Petra loas.*"

"Erzulie, Ogoun, Legba, Damballa," Léopoldie intoned, "all came to these islands aboard the slave ships. And they say other spirits were already here, old Carib spirits—waiting. Nothing has ever been able to drive them out."

Anita said, "Then they must fill a legitimate need," and drank her rum punch.

The old planter scowled. "Its practitioners say it is a legitimate religion. If there is a central tenet, it is that there are two worlds, the world of ghosts and our world, the world of the living. The spirits of the dead are able to visit the world of the living, to bless them or curse them. The wizards claim the power to put the living in touch with the dead, by calling upon Legba to open the door between worlds. If you want the dead to bless you and not curse you, it is essential, of course, that you know their desires."

"Just another damn priesthood," said MacLeish. "World'd be a better place if every clergyman in it was at the bottom of the Cayman Trench."

Léopoldie gave him a really-now look, and Anita tried to inject a note of levity by asking, "Is that on top of all the politicians you want to consign there?"

MacLeish ignored the question and said, "Every time I come sail these islands, I hear people beating on those old drums, and hear about the world of spirits. In the States we have all these persistent stories everyone has heard, thinks *could* be true, wants to believe. Flying saucers, Bigfoot. John F. Kennedy and Elvis Presley faked their own deaths. Planes and ships are swallowed up in the Bermuda triangle. Alligators infest the sewers of New York City. Urban myths. Here I guess you'd call them island legends."

"I would call them arrant nonsense," Léopoldie said, perfectly earnestly, "but it is true, they persist. The *loas* will not go away. I have lived in these islands all my life and heard all of the stories. How, when a man died suddenly, it was because someone had sprinkled chicken blood on his doorstep. How someone took revenge on his enemy by turning him into a *zombi*. How the countryside was terrorized by the *loup-garou*, or, if it was not the *loup-garou*, the *soucouyant*, then, or the *zobop*. How a ball of fire ran along the ground like a thing alive and chased somebody to his doom. Ignorance and imagination are a terrible combination."

MacLeish smirked over the rim of his glass at Anita. She said, "I think for most people belief in something is better than belief in nothing. An explanation is better than no explanation at all."

MacLeish's smirk broadened into the familiar grin. To Léopoldie he said, "She's been to college."

The planter, however, was taking her seriously. "Then why not the *real* explanation?" he said. "We have schools, science, medicine. The Holy Church has been here for almost five hundred years. Yet the people still buy remedies from witch doctors and believe their superstitious fables. Papa Bois is still master of the forests. Hunters still look over their shoulders in fear of him."

"Perhaps," said Anita, "this Papa Bois is comprehensible to them in ways sciences can never be."

"The problem," Monsieur Léopoldie said, touching a fingertip to his temple, "is that education does not penetrate blacks' thick skulls. And the mulattoes are even worse. They have one foot on the church step and one foot in the magic circle. You can always depend on the blacks to be stupid and childish, but you can never be sure what mulattoes will do."

Anita felt her facial expression petrify. She had never in her adult life been so sheltered or deluded as to imagine that racism was not a fact of life in the United States. One of her most vivid childhood memories was of the expression of pride on a real estate agent's face as he assured her parents, "This is a real good neighborhood, folks, there're no niggers here." She had had no idea what niggers might be, but the weight of loathing the word bore impressed her. Afterward, in the car, when she asked for an explanation, her mother shushed her vehemently. Still later, when someone told her what niggers were, she was disappointed. She had expected monsters. Even so, the United States was big— one might see videotape of police officers beating a handcuffed black man on the evening news, or of pathetic skinheads biting themselves in an excess of racist exasperation, but one could live in a nice place, with neighbors who were as nice as oneself and very much like oneself for all that their skin color was different, and come to believe that racists lived only in some other, less-nice place.

Martinique was small....

She made herself relax her grip on her glass. She looked from Léopoldie's face to MacLeish's. He calmly drank his punch. Then he sat forward in his chair, and Anita knew that he was about to swing the conversation around to some topic that suited him.

Later, as they prepared for bed in the planter's guest quarters, she gave MacLeish a bitter look over her shoulder. "The man's rabid," she said. "He fairly foamed at the mouth when he got off on stupid blacks and treacherous mulattoes." MacLeish only grunted noncommittally, and she heard her own voice sharpen. "Or weren't you paying attention?"

"What should I have done? Politely told him that that kind of talk upsets my lady friend? These islands are his home, you're a guest in his house. He's a bigot, okay, but he's sitting on his own porch, drinking his own liquor. He's perfectly within his rights if he wants to say terrible things about people of color—or about women, Old Glory, or the Dallas Cowboys, for that matter."

"And I'd've been perfectly within my rights if I'd got up and walked out."

"Where'd you have walked out *to?*" He flashed the grin. She hated him in that moment. She wanted to put her fist right in the middle of his teeth. "Can't just hail a cab here and say, 'Drop me off in front of Dallas.'"

"Go to hell."

The grin remained in place, but his face hardened around it. She backed off. She was too tired, the rum punch was catching up with her. She pressed her hand lightly against his chest, patted him once or twice, started to move away. He slipped his arm around her and pulled her close. He was still grinning, and she noticed now that he was in a semi-aroused state. She said, "I'm not in the mood," and tried to pull away again. He proposed to get her into the mood. She said, "I'm sorry, Mac." He tried to get her on her knees in front of him and told her she knew how to show him just how sorry she was. She had a vision of herself careering through the halls of Monsieur Léopoldie's mansion, hair streaming, eyes wild, mouth full of MacLeish's blood and meat, the whole household in an uproar. *That* sorry, she thought, as she wrenched away from him and retreated to the bathroom.

She had to come out eventually. He's my goddamn ride home, she reflected angrily. She made a vaguely conciliatory sound as she crept into bed, and he answered with a grunt. They slept with their backs to each other, not touching. She got through breakfast with their host on the strength of her second-best smile, but she was dismayed when she realized that they were to be Monsieur Léopoldie's guests throughout the day. The planter led them on a grand tour of his estate and extolled the beauty of the countryside. A full day in the crossfire of his and MacLeish's bonhomie left her feeling battered by that evening, she was down to third-best smile.

MacLeish evidently did not notice, let alone mind, that she had barely said a word to him or anyone else all day.

The next morning, they sailed from Fort-de-France. Aboard *Martha Ann*, only Burgett was happy. Throughout an interminable predawn farewell breakfast with Monsieur Léopoldie, Anita had spoken only when addressed, which was rarely. MacLeish must have noticed at last that she was out of sorts about something. Up the coast, he opened conversation by pointing out the killer volcano, unrepentant Montagne Pelée; it looked thoroughly pleasant, a green mountain with clouds snagged on its peak. Unimpressed, Anita adjusted her sunglasses, tilted her head back, closed her eyes. The Caribbean sun was hot and brilliant.

"Try," she heard him say, "please just try not to be so intolerant of my tolerance of someone else's intolerance. I do business with the man. When you do business with people, you don't play political-correctness cop with them. You nod, say uh-huh, and get them to sign where you want."

She opened her eyes and glared up at him. "You do business with *me*." She gestured furiously, all-encompassingly with her arms. "Was all this just your way of getting me to sign where you wanted?"

"Oh, Christ, of course not." He angrily turned his back on her. She closed her eyes again.

So much for possibilities, she thought.

The channel crossing north of Martinique was rougher than anything she had previously experienced aboard *Martha Ann*. The sea steepened until the boat clung to the side of a moving cliff of water. Anita had both hands around her favorite stanchion, but the deck kept dropping out from under her, then coming back up in a hurry. Something banged her sharply on the hip one time, and she had the breath knocked out of her the next. A smother of white water broke over the lee rail, sending spray across the deck with stinging force. It went up her nose, down her throat, blinded her, sucked at her clothes as it fell away. She lost one shoe and almost lost her grip on the stanchion. When her vision cleared she glimpsed MacLeish's face; he looked supremely happy and confident as he bawled orders that Burgett could not possibly have heard above the roar of the wind.

She could not say how long the crossing lasted. They were suddenly, finally, in the lee of the next island. MacLeish sagged over the wheel spent and happy. Burgett was looking about tiredly and shaking his head. *Martha Ann*'s canvas drooped in tatters. The jib hung crazily. After a minute or so, MacLeish said, in a croaking voice, "Everybody all right?"

Burgett stumbled aft. "Never saw it so rough as just now."

MacLeish grunted agreement. "Talk about survival conditions." He surveyed the mess of *Martha Ann*'s rigging, then looked ahead, where a landmass loomed over the cracked jib. Anita waited. Burgett kept looking around; he seemed puzzled. MacLeish continued to stare ahead. Nothing moved in his face. His mouth was open.

"Here, Mac," said Burgett, "this is odd...."

"Mac?" said Anita.

MacLeish blinked. His nostrils twitched. He closed his mouth, swallowed. His head began to turn slowly toward the direction of their voices while his eyes tried to stay fixed on the island.

"Mac, what's the matter?"

He blinked again. His eyes met hers briefly. His jaw muscles worked, and from someplace deep inside him came a sound, "Nothing."

Burgett could not be still. He kept moving from one side of the boat to the other. "What the hell is this?"

To MacLeish, Anita said, as lightly as she could, "Don't give me that. You look—"

"*Nothing!*" MacLeish struck the cockpit trim with the side of his fist.

Behind him, Burgett murmured, "It can't be."

"What're you two *talking* about? Tell me!"

"Go below, Anita! Go see how things are below!"

"Don't yell at me like I'm a deckhand!"

"Anita! *Do it!*"

She did it. Water squished underfoot; *Martha Ann* had not been swamped but had been soaked. The gimbaled stove was twisted on its mounts. Lockers had dumped their contents. On her way back topside, she found Burgett at the radio set. He did not look at her as she passed. He had on the earphones, and he plainly was not enjoying whatever he was hearing.

"It's wet and untidy below," Anita told MacLeish, "but as far as I can tell we aren't sinking or anything. Now if you'd kindly just tell me what's wrong—"

MacLeish sucked in a great breath. "Well, I don't know what's wrong."

"But something *is* wrong, is it not? God, I feel like I'm in a Monty Python routine all of a sudden."

"We're *lost*, okay?"

"How can we be lost?" He did not answer and went on looking at the island. She looked at it, too. It was an island like every other island. She said, "What happened to navigating by sight, island to island, the way you—"

Burgett came up. He was even unhappier than before.

"Well?" MacLeish demanded.

"It's bloody panic. Lots of people on the air, calling for directions. I can't get anything from Montserrat, but I'm picking up traffic from Grenada! Nobody's making sense."

MacLeish chewed his lower lip. He shushed Anita when she started to speak and gestured vehemently toward the island ahead. "That should be Dominica," he said, "or it could even be Guadeloupe or Marie-Galante if we were way, *way* off course. But it's none of them! Don't you recognize that harbor? We sailed out of it a few days ago."

"I don't underst—"

MacLeish jabbed the air with his finger. "There's the old fortress, remember the old fortress? It's St. George's! We're off the south coast of Grenada! We're off "

"What?"

"God*dammit*! St. George's! Grenada!"

"I don't understand."

MacLeish laughed harshly, mirthlessly. "You think *I* understand?"

"We're back where we started?"

"A mirage," Burgett said.

"How can it be a mirage?" said MacLeish.

"How can we be back where we started?" said Burgett.

No one spoke for a time. The boat drifted. Then MacLeish said, "The compass needle still points north. The wind and waves are right." Something like a hopeful tone crept into his voice. "Presumably, the sun still rises and sets."

"We can't just sit out here on the water forever."

"She's right," Burgett said. "The boat's banged up. We have to go somewhere."

MacLeish straightened himself behind the wheel. "Okay, okay. Okay. We'll go ashore at—here. We'll find out what's going on, and we'll fix the boat."

Burgett hesitated, nodded, moved forward. They got some sail up, and *Martha Ann* entered the harbor of St. George's, Grenada. A small crowd had collected on the marina. Anita saw people gesticulating and heard voices raised in fierce debate. Two sailorly old men were arguing indiscriminately with each other and onlookers. When *Martha Ann* was tied up, MacLeish, grim-faced, unobtrusively produced two revolvers from somewhere and gave one to Burgett, who barely glanced at it before thrusting it into his trousers pocket.

"Get the jib repaired as soon as you can," MacLeish told him. "We may want to clear out of here in a big hurry. I'll see what I can find out at Government House. Somebody there'll know what this is all about."

With Anita in tow, he brushed past the dispute on the marina at a brisk walk. The old men were arguing in their island English, speaking so rapidly that she could barely understand them. Whatever had started it, the argument had come down at last to who was crazy and who was not. MacLeish hailed a taxi, and after telling the driver to go to Government House, he said, "Anita, I think you should go wait at the hotel. Get a room if you can. We may—"

She shook her head. "If it's all the same to you—"

"We may be here for a little while, and you'll be safer at the hotel."

"Safer than at Government House?" She looked out the window. Away from the marina, St. Georgians went unconcernedly about their business. "Safe from what? I'll *feel* safer if I stick close."

She thought he would argue with her, but he merely shrugged.

"Mac?"

"Mmm?"

"What do you think is going on here?"

He examined the backs of his hands, turned the palms up, tried to shape something in the air between them. Then he let them fall and said, "Beats the hell out of me."

They said no more until the car had made its way along the road around the harbor and entered the shadow of Government House's gingerbread façade. MacLeish told the driver to wait. They hurried inside and found a small, mostly Caucasian crowd there. A pink-faced man at the head of the room was telling everybody to stay calm, the situation was well in hand, please go home. "And what situation would that *be*?" someone demanded in a booming American voice.

The Government House man looked harried, but his very British voice resonated in the room. "We are assessing the situation. As soon as we—"

"I thought you had it well in hand, or is this some other goddamn situation you're talking about?" and with a gesture of disgust the speaker abruptly turned out of the crowd. He almost collided with Anita. He was a thickset balding man with a pair of dark sunglasses pushed up on his forehead. He peered for a moment, then said past Anita to MacLeish, "Don't waste your time here. Idiot doesn't even know which situation he's talking about. MacLeish, isn't it?"

MacLeish, obviously at a disadvantage, only nodded.

"Name's Mitchell. I flew you in last week."

"Ah? Oh."

Anita thought, Only last week...?

"They don't know anything here," Mitchell said. "Only thing they can say is, 'All communication with the mainland's cut off, please go away.' Hell, all communication with most of the other islands is cut off!" As if unconvinced that he was already speaking loudly enough to be heard by everyone in the room, he raised his voice. "Barbados, Trinidad and Tobago, Dominica, the Leewards— it's like they all just ceased to be!"

"All *I* know," said a man in full tourist plumage, "is I have to be in New Orleans tomorrow morning!"

"Maybe New Orleans has ceased to be, too," said someone behind him.

"Maybe it's World War Three," said someone else, and at least two other people moaned.

"Who against who?" snarled Mitchell.

A fiftyish woman dug something out of her purse and advanced tentatively. She held up a pocket-sized New Testament. She said "In Revelations, it says," and no more, because Mitchell said, "Give me a goddamn break, people," and swatted the little book out of her hand. It flew past Anita's head like a mutant bird.

"Really, now, Mr. Mitchell," the pink-faced man began, "Until we know precisely—"

Mitchell ignored him and said to MacLeish, "Walk down with me, I need a drink."

Anita saw MacLeish give the man a wary look. "We, uh have a car waiting outs—"

"Good, then you can give me a ride down. I really need that drink. This thing, event, phenomenon—whatever it is, I can't think about it sober any more. I made my regular hop in yesterday, and everything was normal. I made the hop out of Grenville this morning, heading up-island, and just cleared Martinique when, suddenly, what the hell, I'm approaching Grenada again—from the southeast!"

"I," said MacLeish, "we," and Anita finished for him, "Were on a boat, the same thing happened to us on a boat."

"Everything was normal," said MacLeish, "except—"

Mitchell nodded, turned his palms up, laughed nervously. "Yeah. *Except.* When I saw St. George's up ahead, I turned around and flew down-island a bit and wound up over Martinique again. I got a little crazy then, and who can blame me? I flew west and came up on Martinique from the *east.* Look, some of these folks were on my plane today." Several people in the crowd nodded. "So if I'm crazy, they're crazy, too. And if they're crazy, then everybody on this whole goddamn island's crazy. This is happening to everybody."

The nodding immediately stopped. It struck Anita that no one wanted to agree that this was happening at all.

"The whole time," Mitchell went on, "I was picking up just the weirdest crap you ever heard on the radio. Some guy on a cruiser was crying into the mike about sailing east from St. Vincent for Barbados but coming up instead on St. Vincent from the west. Picked up another boat, this guy says the skipper's jumped overboard, there's all this screaming in the background—" He looked imploringly at MacLeish. "I could use that drink now."

"Mr. Mitchell," the pink-faced man called out behind them, "I can't have you alarming citizens with improbable tales and irresponsible suppositions."

"Hey, pal," Mitchell replied over his shoulder, "I think the appropriate response to what you can't have is, 'Sod off, you fatuous git!'" He flashed a grin at Anita and said, "That's Brit for, 'Fuck you, asshole,'" and she thought, Oh, great, another MacLeish.

They wedged themselves into the rear of the car, with Anita in the middle. Mitchell regarded them intently. His jowls and forehead glittered with perspiration, and his breathing was harsh. He gave the nervous laugh again and said, "I tell you I need that drink. You need one, too, believe me. Everybody on the island's gonna need a drink when they hear about it."

Pedestrian traffic increased as they descended the hill from which Government House overlooked the town, until their progress became a succession of fitful starts. "Man," said the exasperated driver, "you think it was festival the way people walk in front of you."

Is anything ever so terrible, Anita asked herself, that a shower can't make it at least a little better?

Mitchell had quit their company immediately upon arriving at the hotel with the declared intention of heading straight for his favorite bar and getting drunk in an awful hurry. She could imagine him sitting at a corner table, using his hands to recreate or invent an aerial dogfight for the edification of equally drunken companions—Ned and Ted, perhaps. Now who were Ned and Ted? She could not remember immediately.

Anita sat at the vanity table, combing out her hair. She had expected to want to fall asleep as soon as she showered; instead, she was wide awake, wired, in fact, waiting for some sense of strangeness to penetrate. She had watched the sun go down over the Caribbean and seen the first stars come out. What was it MacLeish had said on the boat? The compass needle still points north, the wind and waves are right, the sun still rises and sets. How, then, could anything possibly be wrong? How could they be so *impossibly* wrong...? While I'm sitting here blow-drying my hair the world can't have changed somehow so that wherever you set out from, in whatever direction, you end up back at your starting point. It's too, I don't know, zen or something.

She tried to force acceptance on herself by thinking about Dallas. I have a real life, I own my own business, I make money, I used to be married to a man named Roger, I keep fit, I...

She did not miss it and could not mourn it because she did not believe that it was actually threatened. Surely this was all a mistake, a hoax, an elaborate practical joke....

While I'm putting on my panties, bra, skirt, blouse, while I attend to normal, routine matters like lipstick, the world can be only the world, the world can only be the world.

MacLeish came out of the bathroom. He sat down on the end of the bed opposite her and said, "Here's what we'll do." He looked and sounded like himself again. He had been uncharacteristically quiet ever since *Martha Ann* put in. He had seemed shrunken next to Mitchell. "We're going to get out of here. As soon as the boat's fixed, we'll press on."

She looked at him in surprise. "Press on to where?"

"Venezuela, maybe the A-B-Cs. Someplace."

"I think we're better off to wait and see what happens next. Maybe this thing isn't permanent. Maybe they'll fly in help from the, you know, the outside."

MacLeish frowned. "Maybe there isn't any outside. Maybe the rest of the world doesn't exist any more. Maybe it's all been, I don't know, segmented, partitioned. Maybe there're all these little strips as long and wide as the Windwards, and everybody's going around and around in them and getting nowhere. Or maybe the islands from Grenada to Martinique are the only part that's been cut off. Maybe the gap closed, maybe, back in the world, now you can go directly from Tobago to Dominica. This is all so insane. All I know is, if there's a way out, I intend to find it."

"That man Mitchell couldn't find it, and he had an airplane."

"Maybe it takes a more delicate touch."

She had a vision of the three of them, MacLeish, Burgett, herself, on *Martha Ann*. In the vision, she was a blurry object tucked out of the men's way, and the men were absolutely content, so long as one had his sails to tend and the other could hold the wheel and grin like Ernest goddamn Hemingway, to sail forever and never touch land. She picked at a particle of lint on her robe. "This is too weird for me to have to deal with and worry about drowning at the same time."

"What?"

"If you press on, as you call it, I don't think I'll go with you. I can't tell you what I make of all this, because I can't make anything of it yet. I haven't started believing anything's really wrong, except that everybody else is very upset. I guess I will be, too, if it lasts long enough. For now, I'm just going to play it safe."

"Safe?" MacLeish's frown intensified. "Things are going to get bad in a hurry if this thing doesn't change back. Fragile island economies will be reeling, governments will collapse."

It came to her unbidden, from what felt like a long time before. "They grow everything good to eat here," she said, "orange, banana, pimento, cacoa for chocolate." And smell that good smell. "I've got my credit cards and some cash."

"The only thing cash'll be good for is tinder. Plastic won't even be that useful." MacLeish's frown evolved at last into a glower of exasperation. "These islands, you know, they were infested with cannibals once upon a time. They could be again."

"I'm a big girl, Mac. And like the lady says, a woman today's like an aerialist between trapezes. I'll catch hold of something."

"Goddammit, Anita, down here, you're reduced to just about one marketable skill I can think of."

She had finished dressing. She tucked her handbag under her arm. "One day soon," she said evenly, "I expect to think back on how I let you touch me, and shudder with horror," and tossed her room key onto the bed as she walked out.

The hotel bar was full of people and conversation. Everyone was drinking too much and talking too loudly, and their voices all had the same hysterical edge. Anita ordered a drink. A nervous young man nearby was saying to a glum young woman, "If the plane heads one direction from Grenada only to come back to Grenada from the opposite direction, is it still Grenada? I mean, is this where we were this morning? Is it really the same place?" The young woman rolled her eyes and told him to shut the hell up and get her another drink. The young man ordered another drink for her but did not shut up. "If the plane takes off again and I stay here, will I greet myself stepping off the plane when it gets back?" He noticed Anita and said to her, "Everybody here's got a pet explanation for the phenomenon. Speculation's running strongly in favor of devil's triangles and mischievous extraterrestrials. Me, I think maybe time-space has swallowed its own tail. Any ideas on the subject?"

The bartender set a drink before her. Anita touched the glass with her finger and thumb and watched light sparkle on ice. "An old man shook a stick," she said.

Internationally Unknown

Steven Utley

From 1952 into 1954 my Air Force family lived in southeastern
England, and, from 1959 into 1961, at Naha Air Force Base,
Okinawa. My memories of Old Blighty are vivid, albeit fragmentary
– a little kid's memories. The only remotely literary thing that
happened to me there occurred on my very-first-ever day of school:
I watched and listened, awestruck and appalled, as the other
children recited the alphabet in unison, from memory. I distinctly
recall thinking, in utter panic, *I have to learn all that?*

As for Okinawa, had I known at the time that I wanted to grow
up to be a writer, I would have paid a whole lot more attention
to my surroundings, and taken notes, and then one day written
a terrific novel stuffed with local color – like, for instance, Sarah
Bird's[1]. Ms. Bird, also the product of a peripatetic childhood in
an Air Force family, clearly did pay attention during her own Far
East sojourn; I was far too busy being being a ten-, eleven-, twelve-
year-old boy castaway on an island just brimming with venomous

---

[1]   *The Yokota Officers Club*, by Sarah Bird. New York: Alfred A.
      Knopf, 2001.

fauna and unexploded ordnance left over from World War II. But I did somehow get a poem published in the school newspaper. This evidently inculcated in me a love of the sight of my name in print — even smudgy mimeograph print — and seems also to have set me inexorably on the path to wherever I find myself today.

Not too long after I started writing professionally, I signed on with a West German literary agency. Soon afterward, I beheld for the first time my deathless prose as rendered into another language, when I received an anthology called *Die große Uhr*, edited by Wolfgang Jeschke and containing something called "Custers letzter Absprung." I thought it was pretty nearly about the swellest thing I had seen since my first sight of my own name in print back on Okinawa, and never mind that I don't read German beyond what I encounter in *Katzenjammer Kids* comic strips ("Mitt dos kids society iss nix!").

In due course I found my by-line adjoining such story titles as "Moches de Nuit," "Subito," and "Damals auf der jungen Erde." Two different Italian translators had a go at a tale called "Upstart" during the same year, one rendering it "Il parvenu" and the other, "Al cospetto degli Sreen." "Upstart" is "Uppkomling" in Swedish and "Tsaboukas" in Greek; I like just looking at both of those words. Several other titles, including that of an unauthorized translation of mine 'n' Howard Waldrop's "Black as the Pit, From Pole to Pole," have been rendered into Japanese characters I don't know how to reproduce here, and there are also some in Dutch, Spanish, Portuguese, Russian, and Czech. There are even some in British English. I loved the idea of being in print in the United Kingdom and didn't mind *too* much about being pirated in Japan; because, undoubtedly, of the time I spent in those places during my impressionable childhood, I am somewhat of an Anglophile and a Japanophile.

I've also developed a soft spot for Australia, even though I've never set foot upon nor even come within sight of the place, and know only so much of the language as can be gleaned from movies, television commercials, and hearsay, e.g., "G'day," "beah," "put another sheila on the barbie," and my favorite, strong language reserved for those occasions when mechanical or electronic devices don't work as they should: "The f**king f**k won't f**k!" At least, I'm told that it's Australian in origin; it certainly doesn't seem like something you'd hear fall from the lips of, say, an irate Canadian, assuming you found one.

Anyway, I love Australia because it put me, so to speak, on the map. My first story collection, *Ghost Seas*, was issued by Ticonderoga Publications, out of Nedlands, which I understand to be on the *far* rim of Down Under, the side washed by the Indian Ocean. Could I have ranged farther afield in search of a publisher willing to lose money on a book by *moi*? Not unless there's a small press operating out of Little America.

Actually, it was Ticonderoga, in the person of Russell Farr, who ranged far afield in search of an author on whom to lose money that could have been more profitably ploughed into liquor, lottery tickets, and loose and crazy women. But the tale tells better the other way, and the point is, I finally became *the* author of *a* book all my own. Family members regarded me with fresh respect tinged with suspicion ("Is this book about us?"), and a landmass I had theretofore admired chiefly for its exotic marsupials and its tradition of eloquent profanity shot straight to the top of my list of favorite remnants of the supercontinent Gondwana.

My second story collection, *The Beasts of Love*, came out from the Oregon-based Wheatland Press, but is actually printed in LaVergne, Tennessee, literally right across the road from Smyrna, Tennessee, where I am considered to reside. I didn't plan it this way, it just happened.

The first (and, at this writing, only) review I've seen of *Beasts* is by one Russell Farr. Well, it is a small world. I told Howard Waldrop that if I were an Aussie writer living Down Under, my most devoted readers would probably be Greenlanders. He reminded me that a prophet is not without honor, save in his own land. "We are doomed," he said, "to have careers in foreign lands." Howard is a sensation in, I believe, Finland.

My third story collection, *Where or When*, bears the imprint of PS Publishing, based in the United Kingdom — which brings me full circle — but is edited by a guy who lives in South Africa, which also means that my writing career, such as it is, has now touched all the settled continents as well as a select few of your more important islands.

So, you see, though I might joke about being an internationally unknown author, I'd never lie about a thing like that. About other things, yes, but not about that.

Afterword

Michael Bishop

STEVEN UTLEY, a gifted, idiosyncratic and opinionated writer who has gone unsung longer than the masterpieces on an Incredible String Band album, achieves visibility, audibility, and sublimity in this overdue collection, *Ghost Seas*.

Readers unfamiliar with Utley will here encounter his flexible voice in its full range and at several different volume levels, from the wistfully evocative to the deliciously parodic to the bitterly humane.

Note, too, that Utley refuses to limit his talent to any one fiction category, for which reason this cunning sampler features tales of science fiction, horror, mystery, humor, satire, love, and history.

Almost any working writer you can name would be suspender-popping proud to have produced these stories, but, in fact, Steven Utley lovingly crafted them, and Ticonderoga Publications has done a Very Good Thing gathering them for your delectation.

Acknowledgements

Stories in this collection originally appeared in *Ellery Queen's Mystery
Magazine*, *Isaac Asimov's Science Fiction Magazine*, *Louis L'Amour
Western Magazine*, *The Magazine of Fantasy and Science Fiction*, *Mike
Shayne Mystery Magazine*, *Pulphouse: A Fiction Magazine*, *Shayol*, and
the anthologies *Lone Star Universe* (co-edited by Geo. W. Proctor
and Steven Utley, 1976) and *Stellar Science-Fiction Stories # 2* (edited
by Judy-Lynn Del Rey, 1976).

The essay "Internationally Unknown" originally appeared on the
webzine *TiconderogaOnline*.

FIRST EDITION ACKNOWLEDGEMENTS

The publisher wishes to thank

Steven Utley, Howard Waldrop, Michael Bishop, Joseph Troffimoff, Jonathan Strahan, Jack Dann, Sarah Beth Mennie, Grant Stone, Van Ikin, Kate Armitage, Kate Gallagher, Penny Walker, Al Chan, Sean Williams, Jody Gresele, Lyall Griffiths & Tania Griffiths.

SECOND EDITION ACKNOWLEDGEMENTS

In preparing this second edition, the publisher also wishes to thank:

Liz Grzyb, Alisa Krasnostein, Angela Challis, Shane Jiraiya Cummings, the Mt Lawley Mafia, the Nedlands Yakuza, Sue Manning, Grant Watson, Simon Oxwell...

and still, especially you.